BREAKER

A John D. S. and Aida C. Truxall Book

N. A. PEREZ

BREAKER

Foreword and Afterword by
MARGARET MARY KIMMEL

Golden Triangle Books

UNIVERSITY OF PITTSBURGH PRESS

Golden Triangle Books are published by the University of Pittsburgh Press, Pittsburgh, PA

Copyright © 1988 by N. A. Perez

Reprinted by special arrangement with Houghton Mifflin Company

Foreword and afterword copyright © 2002 by the University of Pittsburgh Press

Manufactured in the United States of America

Printed on acid-free paper

10 9 8 7 6 5 4 3 2 1

ISBN 0-8229-5778-7

To Al and Jo Hart

FOREWORD

Reach and toss, reach and toss, there was a rhythm to the work at the mine in the breaker where Pat McFarlane sat beside his brother. "It was very cold. Freezing wind poured through dozens of broken windows . . . Nervous and excited, his fingers scrambled awkwardly into the chute as he fished out the slate." After the death of his father, and in spite of the best efforts of his mother, Pat was forced to work in the mine to help with family finances.

Pat's days actually working in the mine were much different than what he had imagined. The work was tedious and other boys who worked the breaker often taunted the youngest ones. It was terrible for Pat when his brother Cal left the family without a word; then his sister Annie was let go from her job with the Eliots. Now the McFarlane family had only the smallest of wages that Pat made to live on. But even worse were the long hard days of the strike of 1902 when no one knew when the next meal would appear.

In the village of Scatter Patch, living was hard. The mine owners offered little in the way of benefits to the workers; wages were poor and the company store offered no bargains to families just scraping by. Always suspicious of newcomers, the Irish, who had once been the source of ill will, were themselves now suspicious of groups of workers and their families from eastern Europe, Poland, Lithuania, and Hungary. The story of the McFarlane family is the story of many at the beginning of the twentieth century in the anthracite coal fields of eastern Pennsylvania.

AUTHOR'S NOTE

It was while watching a television documentary about the life of photographer Lewis W. Hine, now famous for his wonderful portrayal of immigrants arriving at Ellis Island almost a hundred years ago, that I first became aware of this modest man and of his invaluable contribution, both as an artist and as a social historian.

Sensitive and compassionate, he was deeply concerned with the problem of child labor in this country around the turn of the century. At that time over two million children were slaving in sweatshops, factories, textile mills and mines, working long hours, at low wages, and often under incredibly dangerous conditions. Frequently Mr. Hine traveled around the United States to record and publicize their plight. All of his pictures are dramatic and moving, but it was the blackened old-young faces of the slate pickers, as they crouched in the cold dusty breakers, that touched me the most.

At Eckley Village, in the anthracite region of northeastern Pennsylvania, I learned how miners and their families once struggled to exist, and caught my first glimpse of that odd and powerful structure where coal was sized and sorted. During early research I discovered that the long strike of 1902, which finally forced operators to recognize the mine workers' union, is considered by many to be the most important conflict in American labor history. That made it easy to choose a year in which to set this novel.

One of Mr. Hine's most poignant photographs continues to haunt me. It shows a flock of white birds flying upward, chalked on the wall by a lonely trapper boy as he waited under the ground in the dark. To me it seemed to symbolize a child's right to freedom, a child's need to soar. I believe it was that eloquent image which directly inspired this book.

—*N. A. Perez*

BREAKER

◆ 1

The breaker whistle blew.

Blew and blew and blew.

Pat felt a creeping prickle of alarm. The class had just risen to chant the pledge of allegiance and the teacher's eyes were lifted, not to the Stars and Stripes, but to a row of portraits hanging above the chalkboard. Hand on her heart, Miss Bates wasn't looking at Washington or Lincoln but at the stern, unsmiling face of Edward E. Eliot, the superintendent of the coal company. It was to him, not the flag or the solemn dead presidents, that she daily pledged her loyalty. "One Nation, indivisible, with liberty and justice for all," she concluded, as if she truly believed in the words that she said. "Boys and girls, be seated."

The sound went on and on. Shrill. Insistent. Whispers rustled around the room. Pat saw his sister Annie flash a nervous glance his way. Next to him, Joanna Pawlek twisted her hands in her lap and stared out the window with big anxious eyes.

1

His hand shot up. "Miss Bates, may I please be excused?"

"You may *not*," the teacher told him. "This class will come to order now. You've all heard the whistle blow before."

Of course that was true. The piercing needle of sound was something they heard every day of their lives as it called men to work or released them at the end of a shift. It shrieked the first news of strikes or lockouts or jubilantly announced when the mines were reopening after a layoff. Yet at this early hour on a dismal November morning the three brief blasts, repeated over and over, could mean only one thing. *Disaster.* A fire or a rockfall or a gas explosion. Under the ground where his father was.

"Patrick!" Miss Bates spoke sharply. "You come back here!" but he was out the door and running.

In the schoolyard, a startled cardinal burned up through the mist, crimson streaked bright against the gray. Ahead, the village floated in thick fog. He saw moving shadows, heard voices shouting in alarm and the thud and slam of closing doors. All through Scatter Patch, people were hurrying in the same direction.

Racing along First Street, Pat saw a line of sharp white pickets leap up beside him. It was the superintendent's fence, holding his white clapboard house separate and aloof from the others. THE PALACE, Mam called it. She always spoke of things that impressed her in banner headlines.

"Mrs. Eliot!" The woman surprised him, standing motionless beyond the gate, almost hidden in the haze. "Do you know what's happened?"

She shook her head, coldly reluctant to speak to a miner's frightened son.

Farther on, Mrs. Argy stood at her open door, a small child peering out from behind her skirt. "There's trouble at Number One!" she cried out before Pat had a chance to ask. "The doctor's on his way there now!"

He waved and ran on. Past Gogarty's saloon, a thumping, rowdy place every tipsy Saturday evening but hushed and innocent on this milky weekday morning.

Past Gruber's Hotel, where the foreign-born bachelors lived. Greenies, they were called, or Hunkies, Polacks, Dagos. Local people resented the way they were flooding the patches, more and more arriving every day to threaten the jobs of American men.

Past the company store, where the clerk was locking up to leave.

A blurred figure lagged far behind.

"Wait . . . wait for me!"

"Hurry!" Pat called. "There's been an accident at Number One!" but he felt sorry when he saw his friend's flushed face and heard his heavy wheezing. Peter Eliot's chest was weak, and exertion and damp weather made it hard for him to breathe.

"Bad luck!" Peter gasped, as he struggled to catch up.

Together, they passed rows of small, dull-red houses trimmed with black, and a communal water hydrant where Old Sport, the Noonans' goat, was banging his head around inside an empty pail. Running again, Pat led the way along a narrow lane that twisted through to the other side of town. It was on Back Street that large immigrant families lived in even smaller shacks, two rooms down and one upstairs, with boarders crammed in to help pay the rent.

Peter stopped, holding his side. "The whistle," he panted. "It's stopped."

The sudden, eerie silence was almost as ominous as the frantic warning signal repeated again and again and again.

Through pale streaming air the breaker appeared, a tall wooden structure rising like a set of crooked stairs. It was here the anthracite was cleaned and sized. Usually the building throbbed and rumbled, as heavy machinery within crushed the great shining chunks, whirled broken pieces across revolving screens, and sent streams of rock and coal clattering down the inner chutes. Now, the place stood silent, the slate pickers dismissed.

"It must be bad," Pat said as they passed, "or they'd never shut it down."

He thought that his brother would have gone to the pit head with the other boys. Maybe not. Sometimes when there was trouble Cal disappeared, waiting until it blew over.

Nearby, vague misted outlines took shape: the black mechanism of the cage, stacked timber, dingy culm banks drifting in puddles of fog. A large crowd had gathered; there was the rise and fall of voices speaking a dozen different languages, the wounded sound of women weeping.

"I'll find out what I can." Peter pushed his way through the excited mob, trying to reach his father. The mine superintendent, surrounded by company officials, stood head and shoulders above the rest.

It will be all right, Pat told himself, but his mouth was puckered dry, his heart slamming hard against his ribs. He fumbled in his pocket for his rabbit's foot and then remembered that Ethel Dugan had won it from him at recess the day before. She'd bet him she could strike him out at baseball—and she had. A humiliating moment.

"Looks like your good luck just ran out," she had jeered, wiping her messy nose on the sleeve of her old gray sweater. He had laughed at her then, but now he was scared.

Ellen McFarlane stood apart, a woolen shawl snatched over her shoulders.

"Mam!" Quickly, Pat went to her. "What's happened?"

"Cave-in." She was shivering in the cold.

"What about Dad?"

"I don't know." Loose strands of fiery hair blew around her white face. "They haven't told us much."

"He'll be fine." Pat didn't know what else to say. "He's always come out safe and sound before."

"Except for the broken leg that never mended straight, and a cracked rib now and then, and that rattling cough that won't let him rest at night. Oh, yes . . ." Her bitter voice sank to a whisper. "He's been fortunate, indeed." She asked, "Have you seen your brother?"

Cal was the one she would want with her now, but Pat saw no sign of him in the crowd. "No."

"Where's Annie?"

"Still in school. The teacher wouldn't let us go."

"So you came anyway . . . without your coat or cap. You'll catch your death!"

"I wish I could leave for good and go to work!" Pat burst out. "Cal did when he was twelve . . . and I'm fourteen!"

"We'll not discuss that now." Fiercely, she gripped his arm. "But take a look around you, for pity's sake. Is this what you want for the rest of your life?"

He felt her rage and her fear at the sight of sallow, unshaven men, red-eyed from too little sleep, and terrified women holding babies hastily bundled, everyone straining for news of missing family members or friends.

"Well, I want more for all of you." Grimly, Mam answered the question herself. She let go of his sleeve and pulled her shawl closer to her body for warmth. "I wonder how many times I've waited here, always wondering if one day . . ." She paused and then went on. "But not today, please God. Not *now*."

Mam rarely cried. Angrily she shrugged off sympathy. He didn't know how to comfort her.

Peter was back. "They've talked to Michael Kulik . . . do you know him?"

"He loads coal for my dad," Pat said.

"He says they heard the roof working this morning. Your father sent him to report it to the boss while he went back to warn the others. That's when it all caved in."

"Then Darcy is trapped or buried!" Mam cried. "How many more?"

"Five or six," Peter spoke softly. "Kulik was hurt, but he

wouldn't wait to see Dr. Argy ... he's gone back down with a rescue team. My father hopes it will reach the men soon."

"What if it doesn't? What if they die down there?" There was passion in Mam, in her dark voice and vivid eyes. "Then we'll be told that our men were careless, that the accident was all their fault."

"Mam, *don't*." Pat wished she wouldn't show her raw feelings when Peter had done what he could to help, to reassure her.

"It's the truth! We all know BIG SHOTS never take the blame when things go wrong."

So often things went wrong.

"There's Cal!" Mam held out her arms to a tall, slender boy who was coming their way.

It's about time, Pat thought, but he didn't say so out loud.

Fans pumped fresh air into the gangways below; officials rode up and down the cage, talking and planning, changing strategy from hour to hour, while, hundreds of feet below the ground, volunteers burrowed through tons of fallen rock in a desperate effort to find the missing miners.

For forty-eight hours, during a long gray space of time, Pat and his family huddled at the pit head with the others. Now and then, some would leave to try to eat or get some rest, but when they returned, always hoping for news, nothing had changed.

No one spoke much or wept anymore. Pat was grateful each time Peter came to tell them what he knew, how the team was inching closer to a rescue. Sometimes, choking in

7

the dampness, he stood and waited with them, hoping for the breakthrough.

On the third day, as people sagged under a cold, drenching downpour, ankle-deep in mud, Mr. Eliot pleaded with them to go home. "Please . . . you'll make yourselves ill," he told the rain-soaked men and women and feverish, coughing children. "Believe me . . . we're doing everything we can."

Later in the dull dripping afternoon, a familiar black horse and cart rattled into Cork Lane, followed by bedraggled Ethel Dugan and some other gaping youngsters, while Yap, the Noonans' noisy mongrel, barked shrilly from his yard.

"Oh, look," Annie whispered. "It's the Grim Wagon."

"And it's stopping here," Cal said.

Pat watched as a big, muscular man lifted a body from the wagon in his powerful arms.

"Mam!" Annie wailed. "Come quick!"

But her mother came slowly from the kitchen. Numbly she took off her clean white apron, set it aside, and then opened the door.

"I'm sorry, missis." Michael Kulik's head was bandaged, and there were deep red gashes on his face. Breathing hard, he carried the long, blackened form across the room and laid it on the sofa. "Six good men gone, but he was the best."

"Well, then," Mam said roughly. "It's over."

She was shaking as if she had taken a violent chill. Annie, too shocked to cry, went to her mother and put her arms around her, but the stricken woman did not respond.

Pat wouldn't look at the body. Instead, he stared at the framed wedding certificate that hung on the wall above the sofa, at pink flowers and cupids and ornate golden letters: *Darcy McFarlane and Ellen Callahan, married at Philadelphia in 1885.*

"Until death us do part," his mother had once promised his father in her low, thrilling voice, and she had kept the vow, loving the man in her own stormy way and yet hating the life that they shared. Now the thing she had dreaded most had happened.

Over.

Anguished, Pat turned toward Cal, but his brother was gone.

❖ 2

"**P**at," his mother said. "It's time. Up now, and give your brother there a shake."

Awake, quick on his feet, Pat shook the quilts bundled over Cal, then reached for his own clothes, folded and ready on a chair. January breathed cold through the flimsy walls, and he heard the wind flapping wildly around the corners of the house.

The red-letter day he had longed for had come with a dark edge of sadness. He had always expected his father would walk beside him when he took his first giant step into the tough masculine world of the colliery.

Downstairs, tea was ready in the thick brown pot. Mam handed him a steaming cup. Her face, creased with worry, was fretful in the lamplight.

"I'll be careful," he told her. "I won't get hurt."

"Not today, maybe." She gave him a thick slice of bread spread with strawberry jam. "To think I swore I'd never let you go, and now you're going . . . *gone*."

She never did know when to hold her tongue. Sometimes his father had silenced her with a glance, but Pat would never dare to look at her that way. He resented her gloomy expression, her refusal to share his excitement about going to work. Besides, there wasn't any choice now.

Annie was out of bed, still in her long flannel nightgown, peering at him through a tangle of fine dark hair. "I suppose you'll soon be smoking like the other boys and telling us all what to do."

"As if you'd take orders from me . . . or anyone else."

"She will soon enough," Mam said. "She's been offered a place at THE PALACE. Mrs. Eliot wants a good, quick girl to help out, and she thinks that our Annie will do."

"Do as she pleases," Pat teased. "Same as always."

"It isn't right. Children having to help support a family when they should still be at play."

"I'm thirteen," Annie said. "I'm not a baby. Lots of girls my age are working at the squib factory or in the silk mills," but she was only putting up a front. In spite of snobbish Miss Bates, Annie still liked school and hated housework.

"I always hoped you'd get a decent education . . . learning comes so easy to you two. It's different with Cal . . . the poor boy can barely write his name." Noisily Mam clattered dishes into the sink. "Your dad never knew anything better than this, but I did. I wanted you to aim higher."

Pat wished she wouldn't talk that way. Most women in the patch were glad to have extra money coming in. And even if she didn't intend it, her words seemed to belittle their father.

Cal came slowly down the stairs and ate breakfast in silence. He never did have much to say, and he was seldom in a hurry to go to work in the morning.

"All right, boys." Briskly, Mam handed over the dinner pails. "You'd better be moving along."

With a queer pang, Pat noticed that she had given him his father's tin bucket, only polished up to look quite bright again. For a few minutes the sad ache in him was so painful that he couldn't speak. Then, taking his coat and cap from a hook on the wall, he kissed his mother's cheek. "Wish me luck."

Instead she said angrily, "I *hate* to see you going to that filthy place!"

Annie gave Pat a tight, hard hug. "I know someone who will miss you in class today," she whispered. "Someone with romantic green eyes."

He knew who she meant. But Joanna Pawlek was three months older, two inches taller, big, strong-willed, and Polish. There was nothing romantic in that!

He was keyed up and shivering as he crossed the brittle garden, heavy boots squeaking through a film of fresh snow, Cal following behind.

It was a five-minute walk along the crooked lane that led to Back Street. In kitchens throughout the frozen patch, kerosene lamps burned yellow-warm against the cold winter dawn as dark shapes emerged from the company houses, some moving off in the direction of the shaft, others hurrying toward the tall, lopsided structure that sloped against a fragile morning sky.

The whistle blew. Under frosty stars, loaded coal cars

shuttled up a steep track to a cupola at the top of the building, while dozens of young slate pickers streamed in through the entrance below.

"Wait a minute!" A hard-faced man wearing an eye patch stopped Pat at the door. "You're new here, ain't you?"

"He's my brother," Cal said. "I'll teach him what to do."

"Learn him good, then." The man spat tobacco juice, and wiped his stained yellow mouth on the back of his hand. Poking Pat on the chest with a sharp-pointed stick, he warned him, "I'll be watching you."

Inside, the picking room was a vast, dingy cavern, clouded with dust. Boys were climbing up tiers under the catwalks, taking their places on planks straddling zigzag chutes that plunged from the roof to the floor. Most were between ten and sixteen, but Pat noticed a few elderly men too, and one in his twenties with a badly crippled leg. There was a familiar saying in mining communities, *Once a breaker boy, twice a breaker boy.* It meant that the old or disabled often ended up in the same place where they started.

Gears and chains creaked, clanged, and rattled into noisy motion.

"Sit here." Cal pulled Pat down beside him on a bench. "And pay attention to what I do." Wheels, belts, and pulleys throbbed and vibrated as a wave of coal thundered down from the top house and tumbled down in thick, churning streams. Quickly, the older boy dangled his boot to slow the flow, his bare hands snatching out refuse and dull-colored bits and tossing them into a box beside him.

"That's all there is to it?"

"It's not so easy at first . . . after a while you'll get a feel for it." Cal picked up a mallet and smashed a large chunk into two pieces. "This is bony. Knock off the rock, and throw the coal back into the chute."

Anxious and alert, Pat was eager to begin, but he soon discovered that he was slow and clumsy as he tried to distinguish the good from the bad. "This stuff is going by too fast . . . I can't keep up!"

"The fellows farther down will get what you miss," Cal said. "Just concentrate . . . you can't daydream in here. You might get badly hurt—or worse."

Pat knew what he meant. The work could be dangerous. Cal had had an accident during his first week on the job and lost two fingers; which was why he kept his maimed hand out of sight in his pocket whenever he could. There were gruesome tales of boys who had been mangled in machinery or smothered in coal. A year ago, Mickey Dugan, the best ballplayer in the patch, had played tag around one of the big revolving screens and had slipped and fallen. His mother had never been right in her mind after that.

"Poor Ma's gone round the bend," Kevin Dugan had told Pat after it happened. "She still thinks Mickey's coming home again."

"Ouch!" Something hard nicked the back of his head. Turning, he saw Chester Cezlak grinning at him from a perch higher up. Quickly he reached for a piece of coal to throw back.

"Stop!" Cal grabbed his arm. "They'll want to get you into trouble . . . especially the foreigners. It's always that way with someone new. Ignore them." He nodded toward the platform above them where the picker boss stood on watch. "Look out for Blackie Pyle. Remember, one eye or not, he doesn't miss much, and he'll hit or kick you when you least expect it."

"He's kicked *you?*"

"Plenty of times."

"What did you do about it?"

"Sat on the bruises; what do you think?"

It was very cold. Freezing wind poured in through dozens of broken windows. Even though a steam pipe twisted up the inner wall it was company policy not to waste heat on the young and warm-blooded when every ounce of steam was needed in the mines below. Pat's body was shaking; it felt as if ice water flowed through his veins.

Reach and toss . . . reach and toss. Nervous and excited, his fingers scrambled awkwardly into the chute as he fished out the slate. Every few minutes another blow struck his head or shoulders, distracting and annoying him. He risked another quick look around. Everyone else was intent on the job, the glow from the carbide lamp attached to each oily cap smearing a pale dab of light among thick clouds of billowing soot. In the eerie haze he recognized most of the faces surrounding him: sleepy-eyed Kenny Bowen, tiny Kevin Dugan huddled next to Boomer Gogarty, the albino Noonan twins with their strange white hair and pink-rimmed eyes sharing a bench down below. Francis Shanahan, Will O'Neill, Colin Daly, and others were friends from his neighborhood, boys he had gone to school with. Some of the foreigners he knew by name as well: Alex Pawlek, Pete Zagorski, Steven Semko, Tony Costello,

Isadore Pochka, Chester Cezlak. Why would they want to torment him?

"I said ignore them!" Cal shouted. "If you lose your temper, then you'll likely lose this job, and you can't! Mam's depending on both of us now."

"I know." Another sharp piece of coal struck Pat's ear. "I just wish they would leave me alone."

He worked mechanically, with hands so numb that they no longer felt part of his body. It was hard to see what he was doing, it was getting difficult to breathe. The noise, so tremendous at first, was like a dull gray thunder pressing down. It was no wonder that pickers often grew hard of hearing in the continuous racket.

He thought of his father, who had gone to work in the breaker at Jeddo when he was only eight years old, so small that his dinner pail dragged on the ground. He had spent thirty-four years in the mines with nothing to show for it at the end, but at his funeral Father Reilly said he had gone to glory and would claim a heavenly reward.

"I hope so," Cal had murmured as they knelt at St. Mary's. "He sure never got anything here." It was the last time he had gone to church.

Pat felt a sudden crack of pain, saw dark blood spurting from his grimy knuckles.

"You're letting the bony pass through!" screamed Blackie Pyle. "We've no room for slackers in here!"

"I'm not a slacker!"

Again the stick whipped down across Pat's bleeding hands.

"Nobody sasses me, mister. You're too slow and too lazy . . . you won't last the day!"

"Give him a chance," Cal spoke up. "He's catching on."

"Listen, you dumb, mouthy micks." The man spat out tobacco and swore. "Keep your eyes open and your big traps shut or I'll throw you both outta here."

In spite of the cold, Pat was sweating with anxiety. He was angry at what Pyle had called them, ashamed that he had been singled out and that his brother had had to defend him. He was certain everyone was laughing at him.

"Calm down . . . you're doing fine," Cal said as the boss climbed up the catwalk. "He always comes down hard on someone new."

Reach and toss . . . reach and toss. Thick-fingered, Pat tried to catch up with the endlessly moving river of coal. *Reach and toss . . . reach and toss.* Gray dust filled his lungs, scalded his eyes, tasted sour and gritty in his mouth. Hours later, when he heard the penetrating shriek of the whistle, he realized with a sense of shock that it was only noon.

Boys, eager for the dinner break, leaped down from the hard wooden benches, punching and shoving, joking and teasing. No one spoke to Pat, but he was too weary to care. All he wanted to do was crumple against a wall and sleep for the rest of his life.

"You're not hungry?" Sitting cross-legged with the others, Cal bit into a heel of bread spread with lard. "Never mind . . . you will be tomorrow."

The immigrants sat apart from the rest, but good-natured

insults were shouted back and forth between the two groups. Food was quickly gulped from the tin pails, then cards and dice thrown down on the dirty floor. Through half-closed eyes, Pat saw Alex Pawlek take a harmonica out of his pocket, polish it carefully with his handkerchief, then put it to his lips.

It was the sweetest sound that he had heard that day.

"Half-hour!" Blackie Pyle swaggered by, his stick slashing harshly against the metal buckets. "And you'll be working late again tonight."

There were a few discouraged moans, but no one seemed very surprised. When coal supplies were low the company pressed employees to work longer hours. Miners complained, but in spring and summer, when there was less demand for fuel, they worried about layoffs and not having enough money.

It went in cycles, Pat thought drowsily, around and around. He was spinning in circles, then he was playing baseball in the yellow heat of summer, dashing across cinders after a bright white ball that kept bouncing out of reach.

The whistle blew. A hand seized his collar, jerking him out of friendly sunlight into the hostile darkness of a winter afternoon. "On your feet, lazy boy! You'd better learn to hustle or you're finished."

Already he hated the boss. As Pat headed back to work, Chester Cezlak stuck out a boot and sent him sprawling. Quickly he was up, fists cocked to fight.

"Come on," Cal said curtly. "There's no time for that here."

He was right. Even if Cezlak was ignorant and a fool, Pat knew he couldn't risk getting into trouble, especially on his first day. Angry and frustrated, he returned to the bench.

He was glad his brother sat beside him. He felt a new respect. Cal was quiet, often moody, a complicated person. It was hard to guess what he was thinking or feeling. *Still waters run deep,* Mam said. She had always been softer and more patient with him than with anyone else. At sixteen, Cal had spent four years in the breaker, but in all that time he had never complained about it at home, not once. *And neither will I,* Pat decided, *not if it kills me and it probably will.*

Every time he glanced upward he saw the boss staring down at him from the platform above.

"Stop worrying," Cal told him. "Keep your mind on your work . . . you're doing just fine."

He tried to keep pace, to ignore the stinging lumps that still struck him now and then. Crouching forward, his chest hurting from the strain, he understood how slate pickers often grew round-shouldered from bending in the same position for so long. Jimmie Reese already had a crooked spine. "He's carrying his boy around with him," old-timers said when they saw a hunched back. Pat hoped it wouldn't happen to him.

Noise. Dust. Monotony. He was part of a roaring machine that went on without stopping. It was the longest day of his life and it would never end; he would pick slate forever.

"Pat!" Cal was shouting. "Didn't you hear the whistle? It's six o'clock!"

Walking beneath hazy evening stars, his boots stumbling under him as he dreamed on his feet, Pat felt himself moving homeward in a streaming flow of coal.

In the warm kitchen, he sat dully in a battered tin tub and

felt the bliss of steaming water sluicing over him, his mother's skilled hands kneading his sore, stiffened muscles. During seventeen years of marriage she had washed her husband's back every night after work. It was a ritual carried out in every miner's home; first a man scrubbed off the dirt in a hot cleansing bath, had food, and then rest. In the morning the circle slowly turned again.

"Well, you finally got your way," Mam said. "You're a working man now, and I hope you're satisfied. But I won't have you swearing and acting the roughneck and getting too big for your britches. You're not too big to be licked, and I can do it if I have to."

For some reason she always expected the worst. What did she see in him, Pat wondered wearily, that worried and provoked her so much?

Supper was boiled cabbage with fresh bread. Since their father's death, Mam had grown frugal with food, stretching every penny that Cal brought home. Now, with two of them earning wages and their sister going to the Eliots' soon, it would be easier.

"Your poor hands." Annie, sitting across the table, reached out to touch Pat's raw fingers gently. "They must really hurt. Are you sorry you're working now?" She was always interested in how people felt about things.

Pat stared at his plate, unable to lift an arm, his eyes dropping shut as he sat, too exhausted to speak.

· 3

In a region of northeastern Pennsylvania slightly less than five hundred square miles, almost all the anthracite in the United States lay buried in three major areas, the Northern, Middle, and Southern fields.

Millions of years before, in a lush prehuman landscape, ancient plants had sunk and decayed. Eventually, under heat and pressure, moisture was squeezed out and the succulent vegetation hardened into peat, then lignite, and finally coal.

Pioneers first discovered it at the mouth of a small creek in the Wyoming Valley long before the American Revolution, when hump-backed hills glowed green with timber and numberless fish flashed like silver arrows through clear, sparkling streams.

Soon, blacksmiths picked the *stones that burned* from outcroppings to blaze hot-blue in their forges. In time, a canal system was built and arks floated shining pyramids to market. During the Civil War and after, production boomed as anthracite was recognized as a superior fuel.

Now, dark smoke stained the skies above steel mills and factories, and sweating railroad firemen fed endless buckets of coal into the burning bellies of the trains as they howled across the continent.

In the early days, it was individual men who had taken risks, bought land, and invested money, hoping the rich black rocks would turn into gold. Wisely, they brought in experienced miners from England, Scotland, Wales, and Germany, with the technical skills to help develop an industry. Fortunes were made and coal empires established. Then, troubled by competition, rising freight rates, and unending labor problems, these owners sold out to more powerful interests.

By the turn of the century an era had ended. Few independents were now running the Pennsylvania collieries. Instead, it was the coal-carrying railroads who controlled most of the anthracite region.

Scatter Patch, located in the Middle Field, was one of many mining villages smudged against the mountains around the city of Hazleton. These communities were all much alike: rows of sad-colored houses renting for a few dollars a month, churches, a school, and a company store, sometimes a saloon, sometimes not, but always the eccentric shape of a breaker stacked against the skyline.

In 1902, six thousand boys, many not yet in their teens, worked ten- and eleven-hour shifts, six days a week, in the dust-filled buildings, and Pat McFarlane was one of them.

For two weeks the rhythm of machinery throbbed in his bones day and night. Even when he slept he went on picking slate, and some mornings he felt as if he hadn't rested at all. He could barely remember that distant time when all he had to do was go to school, tease Annie, and help his mother with the chores. But one midwinter evening he was elated as he raced homeward along Cork Lane, too excited to wait for Cal, who plodded far behind.

"What's that you have behind your back?" Mam looked up from the range where she was stirring thick vegetable soup. There was almost never meat at meals anymore.

"It's for you!" Proudly he brought out his pay envelope.

She sat down at the table she had got by saving Larkin soap coupons, and spilled bills and silver out into her apron. "Is this all? You haven't held anything back, have you?"

The excitement vanished. Did she really believe he would be part of a knockdown, lie about his earnings the way some of the other boys did so they could keep a percentage for themselves?

"No, it's all there. Forty-five cents a day for two weeks comes to . . ."

"Five dollars and forty cents!" Annie was always one jump ahead.

Mam carefully counted the money, then handed Pat a quarter. "Here's something for your trouble. Spend it on whatever you like . . . except tobacco, of course. I know you've been smoking on the sly and don't try and deny it . . . but I won't have you stunting your growth. Your grandfather Callahan was fond of cigars when he was just your age and he never grew any taller than you."

Silently Pat took the coin, but he was indignant that she had accused him of going behind her back. It was Cal who smoked upstairs late at night, not he. He didn't care about cigarettes at all; what he really wanted was a Hohner Marine Band harmonica like the one on display at the store.

It was the 10-hole model that Alex Pawlek played during the dinner break. By cupping his hands and breathing the proper way he could make wonderful music—sometimes a drawn-out, going-away sound like a lonely train whistle drifting off down the track or sometimes quick joyful melodies that reminded Pat of a time long ago when Mam had kicked up her heels and jigged light-footed with a baby in her arms. A brother and sister had died as infants, one from diphtheria and the other from fever, and his mother hadn't danced like that in years.

"Let's have a look." She reached for his hands and examined the nails broken down to the quick, the scraped sore knuckles, the blackened fingers still raw at the tips. *Red tops* were something all breaker boys endured until the skin grew callused. "I can see these are getting tougher every day. Hang on to them, son . . . they can't ever be replaced."

Cal had come into the house. As he dropped his pay envelope into her lap she gave him a warm, trusting look, and Pat noticed that she didn't count the money before slipping it into the pocket of her apron.

There was a knock at the back door, and Annie went to answer it. "It's Mr. Kulik, Mam."

"Ask him in . . . don't leave him standing out there in the cold," her mother called to her.

The laborer, his face scrubbed to a radiant pink, seemed to fill the kitchen with his solid bulk. "For you, missis." He thumped a big bag of flour down on the table and then backed shyly away.

"That's very kind of you." The woman was as confused in his presence as he was in hers. She was uncomfortable with all the immigrants who had come into the region during the past few years. She distrusted their thick, gnarled names, the peculiar food and customs, and she felt superior to the hardy, barefoot women. Yet, in spite of her misgivings, she was grateful to the man who had shoveled the coal that her husband had cut. Ever since he had brought Darcy McFarlane home on that terrible afternoon in November, Kulik had taken a special interest in the family, and he always stopped in on a payday.

"Please sit down."

He hesitated, then settled uneasily on the edge of a chair.

"You'll have something to eat, Mr. Kulik?"

"No . . . thank you."

She did not insist. "How is your wife?"

"Not so well. She has never been strong. I hope she will come to this country soon so I can care for her myself."

"Then you mustn't keep buying us things," Mam told him. "You'll need every penny to send over there . . ." She waved vaguely in what she hoped was the general direction of eastern Europe. "We'll manage."

"How?" He was blunt. "The company has been good to you?"

"The company!" She spoke with contempt. "Darcy was loyal to it until the day he died, and what good did it do him or any of us?"

"No benefits, then?"

"Oh, Mr. Eliot came straightaway after the funeral with his hat in his hand to say there was a place for Patrick at the breaker and that his wife needed Annie to help out. We can live here rent-free for a year. So, unless there's a strike or a layoff, I suppose that we'll get along for a while. But shouldn't there be something more, after all those years?"

"Yes, missis," Kulik said. "That's why we need the union here."

Curious, she asked, "Are you a member?"

"Yes, missis."

"Darcy didn't trust trade unions much. He'd seen too many failures over the years, too much bloodshed and violence. He said he was his own man and didn't need a bunch of Socialists to speak for him."

"Socialists? I don't know much about that. But I do know that the president of our union was once a miner himself. That's why Johnny Mitchell wants to make it safer for us, and see that we don't get cheated when the company weighs the coal we cut. He wants us to get fair wages for the work we do."

"Fair?" Mam was skeptical. "That's not very likely. Coal companies aren't very interested in being fair. BIG SHOTS are only interested in making BIG PROFITS." It embarrassed Pat the way she spoke slowly and loudly to the man, as if he were dull-witted or hard of hearing, but it was the way she always talked to foreigners. "They want to make as much money as they can at as little expense as possible. Why should it trouble them if a man gets killed when there are plenty of others waiting in line to take his place? That's how it's always been and nothing will change it."

"I think in time our union will." Kulik's face was hot and stubborn. "One man who grumbles can do little, but a crowd of angry men can make a difference if they refuse to go to work. I believe things will be better for us someday and for these fine young fellas, too. And it is because of this one"—he nodded at Cal—"that I have come. Today in the mine the trapper fell asleep. The boss was so mad! Mr. Davies called that lazy good-for-nothing some bad names I won't repeat. He said he wasn't . . ." He paused as he often did, straining to find the right word.

"Responsible!" Annie was never at a loss. She was a reader, and it amazed Pat how fast her eyes could peel words off a page. She could stand forever in the company store, peering at labels on canned goods and medicine bottles, and he knew she lifted old newspapers from trash barrels so that she could scan them at home.

"*Responsible*, yeah!" The man glowed at her proudly. "That's what he shouted when he let that careless boy go. So I told him that I knew this real good fella, and he said Cal should go see him tonight. A dollar a day they pay."

"A dollar a day! He'll go . . . of course he will," Mam said. "We're very grateful to you, aren't we, son?"

The strange expression on his brother's face wasn't gratitude—Pat was sure of that; and he wondered what it meant. Kulik had done Cal a favor, shown confidence in him. Lives depended on those who opened the underground doors so that trips of coal cars could pass through. If trappers were unreliable and doors weren't promptly shut again, then ventilation to the farthest reaches of the mine might be disrupted and deadly gases accumulate and explode.

"You won't wait," the man urged. "You'll go tonight?"

"Yes, I'll go," Cal said.

"First you wash!" It was the battle cry of a woman who had been at war with coal dust for years.

He had tried to stay awake but had fallen asleep waiting for Cal to come home. Now Pat wakened and saw his brother slumped on the edge of the bed. "Where have you been? You left ages ago."

There was no answer.

"Did you see Mr. Davies?"

Cal sighed. "I saw him."

"What did he say?"

"I got the job." The voice was muffled.

"That's wonderful! When do you start?"

"Tomorrow."

Pat envied him. His brother had moved up another rung. After a few years in the breaker a boy was fortunate to become a trapper. Later he might apprentice to a transportation crew as a patcher, then be a mule driver, rise to a laborer, and at last become a contract miner like their father. "What a lucky break . . . more money just when we need it most."

Cal lay back against the pillows and folded his thin arms behind his head. "I've been thinking about the time Dad took us into the mine and gave us a ride in a coal car."

"I remember!" Pat was wide awake. "It was exciting . . . it was so pitch black down there I thought we'd reached the middle of the earth. Then you got sick and we had to leave. I was so mad at you!" Something occurred to him. "I think Dad wanted us to know what it was like because he was proud of the job he did, not ashamed like Mam."

"Maybe."

"I wanted to work with him one day, didn't you?"

Cal was quiet. Pat said quickly, "It's still hard for you to talk about him, isn't it?"

"Yes."

"He was so smart and so strong. I always thought if something bad happened he would figure a way to get out."

"I hope it was over fast," Cal said. "I can't stand to think of him buried alive . . . hoping to be rescued . . . running out of air."

It gave Pat cold shivers, imagining, hoping it hadn't happened that way.

"Have you ever been trapped someplace in the dark where you couldn't get out?" Cal's voice was faint and hoarse.

"Annie locked me in the privy once when I was little."

"Were you scared?"

"Not very." Pat laughed. "But it sure did stink in there."

Later he wakened again. The place beside him in the bed was empty. Cal was at the window, staring into the snow-speckled night, breathing in smoke from a forbidden cigarette.

◆ 4

Coal had always surrounded him, glittering in dark caverns underground, piled into slag heaps high over his head. Soot grayed the color, roughened the texture of daily life in Scatter Patch.

Yet, as the hard, shining rock clattered past him down the chute, it was more than a natural presence in his life; it was a livelihood. A few months before, he had wanted to work to feel grown up and capable. Since then the job had become essential to help support his family. But lately, during dinner breaks, the breaker boys murmured of troubles at home. Their fathers felt overworked and underpaid; they were suspicious of the checkweighmen employed by the company to give them credit for the coal they cut and resentful of the high prices they were forced to pay for their tools and explosives.

Strike!

Snakelike, the word reared, hissing, out of whispered conversations.

Strike! Strike!

Pat, remembering the hardships of 1900 when thousands of men had walked out of the mines, knew how serious it would be if anthracite stopped flowing again.

His mind was on that and other things as he stooped at his bench in the thick, dirty haze of the picking room.

Often he thought of his father, whose face and hands had been coarsened by tiny black fragments so deeply embedded in the skin that no amount of soap and water could scrub them away.

"My mother cried the first day I went into the breaker," he had once told Pat in his quiet, hesitant way. "Some mornings I was so sleepy that my daddy carried me there on his back."

Those poignant images remained.

Sometimes he had talked of the terrible mining disasters, like the one at Avondale in 1869. A breaker had been built on top of a shaft to save the expense of transporting the coal, and a fire had started below, the flames roaring upward. "There was no way out for the poor devils trapped underground," he said.

A hundred and ten men had been lost, most of them Welsh. Later a law was passed forbidding such dangerous arrangements.

He had also spoken of the Twin Shaft tragedy at Pittston in 1896, where coal pillars supporting the roof of the mine were too weak and gangways too wide. Fifty-eight men had been buried in a massive cave-in. "One of my best friends is still down there," he had said with a sigh. "They were never able to recover the bodies."

When he was a small boy these grim stories had fascinated Pat, but in some deep, troubling way. Now that he was older he understood why. It was only after major catastrophes like these that operators had been forced to make mining procedures safer; yet conditions were still very hazardous.

Then why had his dad refused to join when organizers for the mine workers' union had tried to gain support in the region two years ago? Had he been too worn out to expect much, or just fatalistic like so many others, believing that nothing could change what was bound to happen anyway? Maybe old Father Reilly, ranting from the pulpit, had convinced him that trade unions were evil and ungodly. Yet what kind of God would intend miners to burrow underground as meek as worms and not even try to protect themselves?

These thoughts crossed Pat's mind as he plunged his arms into the lane of tumbling coal, reaching for slate and tossing it away. The job was routine now, and he felt he must be doing it well enough since Blackie Pyle hadn't bothered him much. Yet each shift was like crawling through a long gray rumbling tunnel to reach the fresh air and freedom at the other end.

He missed his older brother's presence beside him. Since Cal had left the breaker Pat had worked with different partners, but Kevin Dugan's laughing fits were contagious, Kenny Bowen was lazy and dozed often at the bench, and Boomer Gogarty, full of schemes and plans, never stopped talking. Finally Pat had paired off with Alex Pawlek one morning, discovered how well they got along together, and had picked slate with him ever since. Alex was calm and steady and tireless, and Pat was surprised to find out how intelligent he was, when the general opinion of the native-born villagers was that foreigners were dumb. His music at dinner break was the one bright spot during the day, and he had promised to teach Pat to play the harmonica.

Most of the hazing had stopped. He had taken Cal's advice and tried not to lose his temper at the tricks or the teasing. Soon most of the boys had lost interest in making him miserable, except for Chester Cezlak, who never gave up, who still stuck out a foot to trip him or dumped coal on him every chance he got. Worst of all was the nickname he'd given him: *Flea,* because of Pat's small size.

He had grown used to the crushing roar of the rollers, the rattle and screech of machinery, the long dreary hours over the chutes, but he still felt the penetrating cold. Even though he wore a heavy coat and cap, and muffled a thick woolen scarf over his face the way the others did, by the end of a shift he was as warped by the chill as an arthritic old man.

"Why don't they fix the windows?" he asked, one raw February day as he rested his back against the wall during the noon break. It seemed strange to him that no attempt was ever made to replace the broken panes.

Jimmie Reese shrugged; he had bronchitis and coughed so much he was usually too exhausted to talk. Bowen was asleep, with his shaggy head drooping on his knees, while Boomer Gogarty squatted on the floor nearby, riffling a greasy deck of cards through his grubby fingers. He usually managed to win a few pennies every day, but Pat was almost sure he cheated.

A stick prodded his shoulder. "You got a gripe, McFarlane?"

It was the picker boss, slipping up as usual from behind. "No, sir."

"You said something about windows, didn't you?"

"If they were fixed it wouldn't be so cold in here, that's all."

Pyle stared up at the gaps as if he'd never noticed them before. "Glass costs money. And you roughnecks would only bust them again."

Yet he didn't sound angry. Encouraged, Pat said, "We could cover up the holes with cardboard. It wouldn't cost anything and it would help keep the drafts out."

The man, rocking back and forth on his heels, frowned as if the problem intrigued him. "Fresh air never hurt nobody," he remarked at last. "Keeps fellas awake and on their toes." With the tip of his boot he nudged Bowen sharply in the ribs, and the boy opened his eyes with a gasp. "But if you come up with any more bright ideas, McFarlane . . . speak right up. Don't be shy."

Pat wondered if he had misjudged him. The boss seemed friendly enough, even interested, and there were plenty of things that could be improved; he doubted if any changes had been made in the breaker in years. "Well, I have been thinking about the dust."

"Dust?"

"There must be some way to get rid of it so we can breathe in here."

Pyle, nodding and chewing a knob of tobacco, said, "And you've thought of something, have you?"

"The coal could be washed first."

"Washed?"

"Sprayed with water, maybe. Before it comes down the chutes," Pat said. "To get rid of the soot."

"Now ain't that clever!" The small uncovered eye burned bright with hostility. Too late, Pat realized he had been trapped into saying too much. Around him boys were staring in surprise.

"Shut up," Francis Shanahan hissed in his ear. "You'll get us all into trouble."

"Maybe I ought to tell the superintendent how you'd like to make some improvements," Pyle said. "Tell him little sister is boo-hooing about the way we run things here."

Card and crap games were suspended. Kevin Dugan giggled the way he always did when he was nervous.

"I'm not a crybaby," Pat spoke up indignantly. "I just know we'd work better for the company if we weren't half-frozen and choked up with dust all the time."

"Well, I don't think I'll mention the matter to Mr. Eliot. Because if he hears about your nutty ideas he'll likely send you off to the loony bin in Hazleton . . . put you away with the rest of the crazy folks!"

Everyone laughed, but as Pyle strode away, his stick striking at the metal pails with a malicious clatter, the smiles quickly disappeared.

"You *are* crazy," Kevin moaned. "Telling him all that weird stuff. He'll think you're a spy for the union."

"I wish we had our own union," Pat said. "I'll bet we'd get the windows fixed if we threatened to walk out."

"Shhhhhhh . . . if the boss hears what you're saying he'll fire you," Shanahan said wildly. "And all the rest of us, too."

"Mike Kulik told me some breakers have junior locals," Pat said. "The boys pay dues and have secret meetings where they talk things over . . . why not us?"

A hand was clapped over his mouth from behind. "I've already been in trouble with the company," Pochka told him, "and this is the only work I can get. So don't let your big ideas ruin it for the rest of us. I'm warning you . . . keep quiet!"

"Hey! The Flea wants the coal washed nice and clean for us . . . ain't that sweet?" Cezlak grabbed Pat's cap and dangled it teasingly over his head. "Come on, Flea . . . jump for it! Bite!"

Pat flew at him and rebounded off the boy's big solid chest. Then he was lying on his back in the dirt with the wind knocked out of him and Chester sitting on his ribs, laughing. "Get off . . ." he panted. "*Get off!*"

With a happy grunt Cezlak heaved himself up, lost his balance, and brought an enormous boot crashing down on one of the dinner buckets. "Oooops . . ." He stooped to pick it up. "Sorry . . . I didn't mean to do that."

"Give it to me!" Pat got to his feet and snatched away the crumpled pail. "Look what you've done! You've wrecked it, *you stupid Polack!*"

The whistle blew. Quickly everyone headed back to the benches.

Pat was ashamed of what he had said, the fury behind it. There was always a lot of name-calling in the patch, but he had never been part of it because he hated it when someone taunted him for being Irish or Catholic. Yet something belonging to his dad had been carelessly destroyed, and he couldn't forgive Cezlak for that.

He felt worse when he saw Alex sitting with another partner and realized that when he had shouted *stupid Polack* at Chester he had offended his new friend as well.

It had been a terrible day. Angry and upset, he took the empty place beside Boomer Gogarty.

"You should fight Cezlak!" Boomer had grown up in a tavern and seen a lot of brawling, but because he had a withered leg he was always promoting contests among the other boys. "I can give you some tips ... I've watched hundreds of fights ... and plenty between my Ma and Pa, too." Excited, he jabbed his snub nose with his thumb and made punching motions with his fists. "We could charge admission and split the profits—what do you say?"

"I couldn't win ... he's twice my size," but Pat's words were drowned out as a new wave of coal was dumped down from the top house. There had to be another way to get even.

Every time he glanced up at the platform in the afternoon he saw Blackie Pyle glaring down at him.

◆ 5

"**P**at . . . is that you?"

Peter Eliot was waiting as Pat came out of the breaker into the cold night air.

"Yes, it's me!" He scrubbed at the dirt on his face with a filthy coat sleeve and laughed. "Can't you tell?" He was happy to see his friend. They had seen little of each other during the past few weeks.

"I've been here for ages. Do you always work this late?"

"Yes, and sometimes later." Pat noticed that other boys, hurrying past, were staring at Peter's handsome camel-colored coat and white muffler, and he knew they were wondering what the superintendent's son was doing there.

"You have to come with me. I have something to show you!"

Peter was like that, excitable and impulsive, especially when he had something new to show off—a game, a pile of adventure magazines, some special place he had discovered for a hide-out. Like Annie, he loved books, and when he and Pat took hikes together he liked to act out the dramatic parts of the novels he had read—become a slithery Fagin from *Oliver Twist* or the obsessed Captain Ahab in *Moby Dick*. Sometimes he talked of going on the stage, even though he knew his parents wanted him to be a mining engineer like his father. He was one of the few boys in the coal patch who would graduate from school, and probably the only one destined for college. It had never mattered much before, but Pat, suddenly conscious of his own dirty working clothes, was now aware of the differences between them.

A snowball caught him on the side of the head as they moved away from the building. There was loud jeering laughter as a group of shabby boys dashed off toward the shacks on Back Street.

"Too bad you have to work with those ignorant foreigners," Peter said.

Pat felt a quick shift of loyalty. What right had Peter to criticize when he had never done a hard day's work in his life? "They're not so bad," he said. "Some are all right ... like Alex Pawlek."

"At least he speaks English." They were cutting across the village along an icy lane. "My dad doesn't think much of the Slavs. He says they're like donkeys, all brawn and no brain. He says they stir up trouble because they don't know their place yet ... they don't understand how we run things in this country."

Pat admired many things about Peter, but he had always

disliked his eagerness to lecture, to assume his point of view was the only one. "Maybe I don't understand, either. Maybe you can explain it to me."

"It's the ones who operate the mines that have the hardest jobs. Because they have to answer to the shareholders if the profits don't come in. And if the coal companies don't make money, then there wouldn't *be* any work."

"So miners ought to be grateful. They don't know when they're well off."

"That's right!" Peter had missed Pat's sarcasm. "Instead, all they do is complain."

"I think it's the other way around. If miners didn't risk their necks then companies couldn't get rich. And the men are treated unfairly ... believe me, I know what I'm talking about."

"Well, let's not argue about it," Peter said cheerfully, his breath streaming out in a thick white cloud. "I shouldn't expect you to understand how complicated the coal business is. That's why it takes educated men to run things. Which reminds me ... someone has volunteered to teach classes at night and my father has given permission. It's to help the foreigners learn English and for boys who have left school early. You should think about signing up."

"I just left ... and I'm not going back." Pat resented Peter's patronizing attitude and wondered if he was jealous because he had been left to sit behind with the girls while almost every other boy his age was doing a man's work. Yet Pat didn't want to quarrel with him. They were still best friends, and he missed spending time with him. He changed the subject. "How's my sister doing over at your place?"

"My father really likes her . . . she makes him laugh a lot. Of course, Mother is pretty fussy . . ."

"And Annie takes shortcuts," Pat guessed.

"Sometimes she picks up one of our books and forgets what she's supposed to be doing. Then she gets scolded and that makes me feel bad."

Peter had always had a soft spot for Annie, but even though he was tall and good-looking, with fair curly hair and bright dark eyes, she had never paid much attention to him.

"I'll talk to her," Pat said. "We need the money at home. I don't want her to get fired." It embarrassed him to have to say it.

"Don't worry, I won't let it happen. If she gets into trouble I'll just kick up a fuss. You know I have trouble breathing when I get upset." Peter smiled. "My parents will do anything to prevent that."

They had come out of a lane and turned into Front Street, their feet crunching over the frozen snow. Men were going into the hotel for supper, or heading toward the warmth and sociability of the saloon.

"Where are you taking me?" Pat asked. "It's getting late . . . I should be going home."

Peter just laughed and turned his collar up against the freezing wind. When they reached his house he stopped and swung the gate open. "Come on in."

Pat had never once been invited beyond the white picket fence, and he doubted if many other people in the patch had either. "I'd better not. Your folks wouldn't like it."

Peter didn't deny it. Their friendship had always had

boundaries. It was understood that Eliots didn't mingle with laboring men but only associated with company officials and their families, who lived nearby in an area that villagers mockingly called Silk Stocking Row. "My parents aren't home," he said, "and Annie and the cook have already left. It'll be all right."

Curious, Pat walked along the flagstone path, up the steps, across a wide porch, and through heavy double doors. Then, in the darkened foyer of the big silent house, he stopped, feeling nervous. "I shouldn't be here."

"Oh, come on." Peter stepped into the front parlor and waved for him to follow.

Pat had a dazzling impression of warm glowing lamps, of shining brass and crystal and silver objects scattered all around the room. There was a crimson velvet loveseat with matching bowlegged chairs and dark gloomy pictures in heavy gilt frames hanging against the red-and-gold flocked walls. Even though Annie had described it over and over in detail, he had never imagined it as quite so splendid.

"Well, what do you think of this?" Peter was at the other end of the room, standing beside a piano. He took off his cap and scarf, shrugged off his overcoat, and threw them in a heap on the floor. "It's called a baby grand. My aunt in Philadelphia died and left it to me in her will. It was delivered this morning."

Pat's boots sank into the thick oriental carpet as he crossed the room and stood gazing down at the curved ebony lines and long gleaming smile of the keyboard. "It's beautiful! Can you play it?"

"No, and I probably never will. I can't even carry a tune . . . but in spite of that Mother has gone to Freeland to arrange lessons for me." Peter laughed and gestured grandly. "Go ahead . . . try it."

"My hands aren't clean."

"Never mind that. I want you to hear how it sounds."

Pat sat down on the padded stool and passed his fingers lightly over the cream-colored keys. For a few minutes he tinkered, enjoying the lush resonance. He remembered a song that Welsh miners often sang on their way home from work in the evening and searched for it, trying out one note after another until he found ones that matched the melody stored in his memory.

> Abide with me!
> Fast falls the eventide;
> The darkness deepens:
> Lord, with me abide. . . .

"That's nice," Peter said. "I've heard my mother sing it. I didn't know you'd played a piano before."

"I haven't."

There was a great, cold thrill building in Pat. He and the instrument were mysteriously connected, wood and wire and ivory combined with some secret deep in his brain to produce . . . what? Not real music—that was a complex language still unfamiliar to him—but something near it. It excited him to know it was in him to learn.

"*Louder!*" Peter urged. "Push down on the pedals and make the notes run together. This thing can really make a racket!"

Happily, Pat smashed down noisy thunder with his left hand and streaked in lightning from the right while Peter thumped both fists heavily upon the lower keys. They laughed as the room shook with the storm, the shining prisms on the chandelier swaying and tinkling overhead.

"What on earth is going on in here!"

Startled, they turned and saw Mrs. Eliot standing in the entrance to the parlor, shock and horror on her long pale face.

"Mother!" Peter fumbled for an explanation. "This is my friend Pat . . . he's Annie's brother."

"I don't care who he is . . . just look at him! The boy is absolutely *filthy!* It's disgusting!"

"He's just come from the breaker . . . I asked him here to see the piano."

"Well, he's seen it. Now he can go." Coldly she turned and left the room.

"I'm sorry." Peter's cheeks were flushed and his chest heaved in an effort to catch his breath. "She was just surprised, that's all. I'm sure she didn't mean to be so rude."

Pat hurried toward the foyer, wishing he had never let himself be persuaded to enter the house. He hated the way Peter and his mother had talked about him as if he couldn't speak for himself.

"Wait!" Peter called after him. "I really am sorry. Don't be mad at me . . . *please.*"

But as he left, Pat slammed the heavy doors behind him. It made him feel better, eased his hurt feelings a little.

He was relieved that Annie hadn't seen him humiliated

that way. Mam mustn't know, either. She'd never get over it, his going to The Palace in his dirty breaker clothes.

Thinking about it made him feel angry, guilty, and ashamed. He would never go back there, not ever.

• 6

Lamps shone inside the company store, called the "pluck me" by the villagers who had to pay the inflated prices. Through the window Pat saw his sister standing at the counter, waiting to be served. Because they both worked long hours they hadn't seen much of each other lately.

The bell rang as he stepped inside. Annie looked his way, her small, fine-featured face bright with pleasure. "Pat! Wait for me . . . I'll only be a minute."

He never minded spending time examining the fascinating mix of merchandise: patent medicines, boots and bedding, hardware and hats, barrels of flour, sugar, and crackers, and a thousand other useful items. Trinkets for children as well, although few could afford them. His father had made most of their toys when they were small, patiently stringing cans and boxes together to construct trains, whittling dolls for Annie and sassafras whistles and slingshots for him and Cal. Then, a few weeks ago, Pat had received the best present of all.

"Your father made this for you," Mam had told him on Christmas morning. "It was to be your special gift."

A bat, fashioned from a piece of seasoned mountain ash, turned on a lathe, shaved and sanded, rubbed as clean and smooth as glass. It hurt knowing that his dad would never see him use it. They both shared a passion for baseball. Pat's love of the game was a deep joy that bubbled up every spring when he and the patch boys played their first game in the pale spring sunshine.

Harmonicas were displayed in a glass case near the front of the store. The most expensive one held his attention for a long yearning moment. It cost two dollars and was way beyond his means, but by the next payday he would have saved seventy-five cents, enough to buy a cheaper model. Alex Pawlek had promised to show him how to play but after what had happened, Pat doubted that he would.

Other customers browsed among the shelves. Dr. Argy smiled and nodded, his gray eyes looking old and tired in his young, neatly bearded face. He was well liked and respected even though it was a hardship for miners to have a dollar taken from their paychecks every month to help pay for his services.

Pat saw Michael Kulik poking through a stack of shirts, the kind the men wore to work with their coarse denim pants. "Too much!" he said in a loud, disgusted voice, and pushed the red plaid garment aside. Two men standing near him exchanged uneasy glances and then moved away.

Pat hoped that the clerk hadn't overheard. Even though

people objected to the high cost of food and supplies, the tools and explosives needed for cutting coal, few openly complained. Men had been fired after Mr. Smythe had reported their hostile remarks to the company management.

Kulik greeted Pat with a wide friendly smile. "How's your momma doing these days?"

"She's well, thanks." Politely Pat asked, "And how is your wife in Poland?"

"No word . . . nothing . . . not in weeks." Helplessly, the big man held up his hands. "What can I do but wait and hope nothing is wrong?" Leaning closer, he said quietly, "Say . . . I am worried about someone else . . . it's your brother."

Pat was surprised. "Why?"

"Cal don't look so good. Long face . . . sad eyes . . . he don't talk to nobody. I got him that job, that's why I feel so"—he paused, searching for the word, and then remembered—"*responsible*. Ask him please if there is trouble . . . if maybe I can help."

"I will, Mr. Kulik."

"We are friends now. Call me Mike."

"You've made a mistake, Mr. Smythe." It was Annie's clear voice heard throughout the store. People turned and stared as she held up the container of kerosene with a potato pushed over the spout to prevent it from leaking.

"I beg your pardon?" The sallow clerk, whose thin black hair was combed forward to touch the top of his eyebrows, had an insolent habit of peering down over his glasses as if he were taller and more impressive than he really was.

"Kerosene . . . it's two gallons for a quarter, isn't it?"

"Correct."

"But see . . ." Annie reached for the ledger and swung it around, pointing with her finger. "You've marked down thirty-five instead of twenty-five."

Smythe snatched the book away. Grudgingly he changed the figures, but he didn't apologize. Pat had never seen anyone challenge his tiny cramped markings before. Except for his sister, who could read upside down!

"He's done that before," she said, when they were outside the store and walking home together. "But I never had the nerve to speak up until today."

"He won't forget it," Pat said. "He'll try to make trouble for you."

"Let him . . . I don't care! He wants everyone to be afraid of him because it makes him feel important, and he's not. I hate the way he makes the foreigners wait until everyone else is served first. He's just a mean little man . . . he's so inconsequential."

Pat laughed. "Now where did you find that ten-dollar word?"

"In a dictionary over at the Eliots'."

"When you should have been dusting, I'll bet."

"You've been talking to Peter, haven't you?" Annie sounded nervous.

"Yes. He wanted me to see the piano."

"You went there?"

"Not for long." Pat's face grew warm, remembering. "His mother came home . . . so I left."

"Oh, isn't she awful!" Annie was indignant. "She makes me feel lazy and stupid and not very clean. I get so upset I'm always dropping and breaking things."

"Try to be careful," Pat warned her. "You know Mam's counting on your pay."

"I know." Annie sighed. "But doing housework is such a big waste of time. It's only when I'm reading that I feel I'm doing anything that matters." She tucked her hand through his arm. "I miss school, Pat. I miss how it was before."

He understood. Until he had gone into the breaker he had never realized how completely work would fill his life. Free time was precious to him now, and to Annie, too.

They turned into their lane. Yap barked noisily as they approached their neighbors' house, and they heard shouting voices, a child screeching in a temper tantrum, the usual ruckus.

"Mrs. Noonan's baby is due soon—her ninth," Annie said casually. Then she laughed. "I think they should call Mr. Noonan Old Sport, instead of the goat."

She often tried to shock Pat by saying such things and sometimes succeeded. This time he laughed with her. "Annie, mind your tongue."

It was late when they sat down to eat. The kitchen was cozy, a copper kettle whispering softly on the back of the range that had GOOD MORNING printed in shining nickelplate on the oven door. Mam had spread a clean white cloth for supper. She boiled and bleached flour bags until they were snowy and then made curtains and tea towels and table coverings, embroidered with cheerful colors in an effort to brighten the house.

"We're almost out of coal," she reminded them as she handed around plates of baked beans, smoking hot.

"I'll go soon," Annie promised. She smiled at her brothers. "Remember when we used to slide down the slag heaps on a shovel?" Even though she had hated those expeditions when the three of them had spent hours sorting through dingy piles of waste looking for usable bits, she had usually managed to have fun doing it. Although the company sold fuel to employees at a cheaper rate, it was still a great expense during a long, cold winter, and most families tried to salvage what they could from the culm or to forage for it along the railroad tracks. Mam was annoyed that the immigrant women and children worked at it longer and harder than the rest, pushing heavy wheelbarrows or dragging big canvas sacks, even though she knew perfectly well that foreign laborers earned less money than native-born contract miners.

Her eyes were on Cal as he poked listlessly at his food. "You're not yourself these days. What's troubling you?"

He shrugged.

"You've hardly said a word about your new job."

"There's nothing to say."

"You don't get paid for doing nothing!"

"When a trip of cars comes through I open a door and close it afterwards. That's all there is to it. Mostly I sit by myself in the dark."

"But that's so boring," Annie said. "It's a pity you can't read down there."

Cal, not eating, leaned his cheek on his hand. "You know I can't read."

No one understood why. When he was small and first learning the alphabet, Miss Bates had ridiculed the way his shaky letters straggled the wrong way or flipped upside down. Discouraged, he had strayed away from school. Yet when he did go to class he could remember later almost word for word what had been taught that day. Cal was a puzzle.

"So how do you pass the time?" Annie wanted to know.

"Sometimes I draw on the walls with a piece of chalk . . . there's enough light from my carbide lamp." The corners of Cal's mouth lifted a little. "I have a pet rat. I've tamed him by feeding him scraps from my dinner pail. Beastley's his name."

"Oooooooh." Annie shuddered, aghast but interested. "I hate horrible rats!"

"You wouldn't if you were in my shoes. They can sniff out trouble first. When *they* run, everyone runs. Beastley might even save a life someday."

"I'd hate to be a trapper." Annie's eyes, light blue and wide apart, were sympathetic. "Knowing that some dreadful thing might happen at any minute."

Pat wished she hadn't said it. "Miners don't think about stuff like that. If they did, they'd go crazy."

"Oh, they think about it all right," Cal said. "They just don't talk about it much."

"It takes courage to go down there day after day . . . but Cal is strong like his father." Mam reached out and touched his thick dark hair. "He won't always be a trapper . . . he could be a driver soon. You'd like that better, wouldn't you, son?"

"I'll never do it!" Cal pulled away from her. "Mules can spend their whole lives underground and never see daylight.

It's so cruel! And sometimes the boys kick and beat and even kill them."

"Dad used to say they were treated better than the men." Pat knew that the first question often asked by company officials after an accident was whether any animals were dead or injured. "After all, it costs money to replace one of them. Miners are easy to come by."

"I'm tired." Abruptly Cal rose from the table. "I'm going to bed."

Pat said, "I'll go up with you." There was something he wanted to know.

"Then please ask to be excused." Mam never let up on correcting their manners.

"I saw Mike Kulik today." Pat yanked off a boot and dropped it on the floor. "He's worried about you."

Cal's voice came from under the covers. "Why?"

"I don't know. Maybe you can tell me."

The figure beneath the quilts burrowed deeper. "I said I was tired. Let me sleep."

Pat finished undressing, blew out the lamp, and crawled between the cold sheets. His brother was breathing heavily, but Pat was almost certain he was still awake.

When they were younger he had followed Cal out in wind and weather to explore the wooded mountain that rose up at the edge of the patch. How silent and beautiful it had seemed, away from the bleak houses and dismal streets, the rumble of the breaker. It was there that Cal was happiest, and completely at ease. During the long, white mystery of winter they would kneel in fresh snow, deciphering animal tracks; in spring and summer they peered into the secrecy of stars and stones and water. In autumn they tramped together through the crackling woods, leaves rustling down around them like a dry, brown rain. Always on the lookout for birds, Cal could identify most of them and mimic their songs.

They had been children then. Now that they were almost grown there was no time for close moments of discovery and friendship. The person lying next to him was almost a stranger.

In the night, Pat woke, heard muffled, wrenching gasps. Cal lay with a pillow pulled over his head, his body shaking. He was crying. *Crying!*

Suffering. But why? Pat broke into a sweat. What should he do? He wanted to reach out and offer comfort, but he knew that Cal would hate him for knowing and would draw away, ashamed. Sad and frightened, Pat lay without moving until he heard one last despairing sigh and the room was still.

◆ 7

Ellen McFarlane was a handsome woman, small and well shaped, with a drift of rich auburn hair and eyes like blazing bits of summer sky. She had been raised in Philadelphia and educated at a convent school; it showed in the proud way she carried herself and spoke and in her efforts to transform what she had into something better. *The candy life* was what she called the sweet affluence of her youth, and she had never lost a taste for it.

Her father, Honey Callahan, was clever and charming and freckled with faults. He had emigrated to America at a time when employment notices often shouted NO IRISH NEED APPLY, but in spite of such warnings he had done rather well for himself. For a while he succeeded in politics. A widower as his only child grew up, he had loved and indulged her and promised her that she would always have the best. Ellen adored him and thought of him then as a witty *bon vivant* instead of a man who spent more than he had and drank more than he should. She could believe he was a scamp but not that he was corrupt.

Before they were wrecked by his troubles, father and daughter went to a popular mountain resort in the northeast. Here, on Saturday nights, dances were open to the public and attracted many people from the region, especially young miners who came from miles away to hear the music and to gaze in admiration at the pretty, fashionable young girls.

At the pavilion, Ellen had waltzed with a bashful bachelor who had shyly called her ma'am, then and ever after. When she returned home he wrote letters that revealed his strong, ardent nature. Flattered, she was quick to respond, and yet she was practical; it was only after her father went to prison for embezzling Democratic party funds and she was left alone that she invited Darcy McFarlane to visit her in Philadelphia. (It would take a year for him to repay the money that he had borrowed for his train fare.)

Once he reached the city he asked her to marry him, but he also told her bluntly what to expect if she did. By then she loved and needed him, and didn't listen hard enough to what he said. Together they returned to Scatter Patch as man and wife.

She hated the place as soon as she saw it, the sight of the breaker staggered against a dirty sky. Outspoken and emotional, she raged against coal dust and grime. Although she would never get things clean enough to suit her, there would always be lace frosting Annie's starched petticoats, white pocket handkerchiefs for her sons, an ivory monogram satin-stitched on her husband's gleaming Sunday shirt. She couldn't control her gloomy surroundings, but her power over her children was strong. Even when they were small she had tall ambitions for the three of them.

Cal's lack of literacy was a blow. She was depressed when he left school at twelve, and even more discouraged when the other two were forced to go to work after their father's death. So, when she heard classes would be taught at night, she told Pat what he was to do.

Obedient, but against his will, he went.

"May I have your attention, please?"

The room smelled of sweat, damp wool, and kerosene. Men, crowded into narrow seats at the back, stopped talking although there was frequent dry coughing; boys continued to laugh, spit, and swear. Pete Zagorski and Isadore Pochka rolled dice on the floor while Chester Cezlak, always clowning, lunged playfully at Alex Pawlek, caught his neck in the crook of an arm, and wrestled him down.

"Stop that!" The schoolmaster gripped Chester by the ear. "This is a place for instruction, not disruption!"

"Ow! Leggo!"

"If you intend to be a nuisance then you'd better leave now, and not come back. Do you understand?"

"Yes."

Red-faced and grinning, Chester pulled free and squeezed himself into a seat. His mother cut his hair by putting a saucepan over his head and trimming around it in a perfect circle, and it made him look comical, like a big beaming baby.

"Yes, *sir.*"

"Yessir," Chester mumbled.

"I will ask all of you not to smoke, chew tobacco, or expectorate. No bad language, please."

Silence.

Satisfied, the young man in the cheap dark suit moved toward the chalkboard. His head, with its keen black eyes and sharp bladed nose, seemed too large and aggressive for the thin, underdeveloped body. "My name is Brian Foley." There was an impressive strength in his voice.

For years Pat had seen that pale face staring out a window in a shabby house at the end of his lane. Foley had had a fever when he was small that had damaged his heart and prevented him from going into the mine with his father and brothers.

"I have volunteered to teach you boys who have had to leave school without completing your education and to help you older men learn to read and write. As for others who are new to this country, who wish to improve your English and prepare for citizenship, I am here to assist you in every way I can."

He paused, glancing among the solemn rows. "We have many differences among us. Our English, Welsh, Scottish, Irish, German, Italian, and Slavic ancestry . . . our various cultures, customs, and religions. Yet we share one thing in common."

"We're all poor," piped Kevin Dugan.

Everyone, including the teacher, laughed.

"Yes, but it is coal that connects us. Coal is money, it is power, it is even political."

"And it is so damned heavy," muttered a deep weary voice from the rear.

"That is true." Foley wasn't smiling now. "It is a very heavy burden on your backs."

Pat yawned, shifting restlessly in his seat.

"What you men do is one of the hardest jobs on earth. To drop hundreds of feet below the ground into darkness, to risk your lives daily by explosives or rockfalls or flooding or poison gases is dangerous, often deadly, employment."

Pat sat up straighter, listening.

"And you younger ones who pick slate in the breaker, who breathe in that unhealthy dust day after day . . . what you do is also undervalued and underpaid."

Sleet slashed across the windows and rattled the panes as the slight man paced back and forth across the front of the schoolroom.

"You miners work longer hours and at greater peril than most other men. If you are paid by the car, the cars get bigger, if you are paid by the ton, the tons get heavier. If you are hurt or die in an accident there is seldom any compensation. If you complain about poor working conditions you will likely lose your job. If you refuse to buy overpriced goods at the store you may be threatened or fired. Join the union and you are suspect, strike and you may be cut down by the Coal and Iron police. Your families suffer as you do. A few operators and rich railroad magnates control thousands of lives."

"Who are you?" a rough voice challenged. "Some kind of union organizer?"

"Sounds more like preaching than teaching," another man spoke out.

"I have no connection with the mine workers' union,"

Foley replied. "And I am not a radical or anarchist or Socialist agitator. I only want to inform you of your rights as American citizens, as working people, as dignified human beings."

From the front row came a sputter of snoring as Kenny Bowen slept with his head on his arms. There was laughter. Brian Foley stopped pacing. "First I'll take down your names for the roll call," he said, "and then we'll proceed."

Pat thought over what he had heard. Miss Bates had drilled into her pupils that they should be grateful to the company for providing jobs and housing, a doctor and a school. This message was entirely different. Did Foley really believe that illiterate miners and ignorant boys were as important as bosses and rich financiers?

The idea excited him. He wanted to discuss it with Cal. Maybe he could persuade him to come to the next class.

Later, at dismissal, Alex Pawlek touched his arm and handed him a folded slip of paper. "My sister asked me to give you this note."

Curious, but embarrassed, Pat shoved it into his pocket. He hadn't thought of Joanna in weeks and had no idea why she would write to him. "Alex!" he called as the other boy headed for the door. "I'm sorry about what happened at the breaker. I'll never call anyone that name again."

Pawlek nodded. "I'll see you tomorrow," was all he said, but Pat thought he heard something in his voice that suggested they might become partners again.

"What's that?" Annie sat by the warm range poring over a newspaper that she had brought home from the Eliots'.

"A letter."

"Who sent it?"

"Why don't you tell me?" Teasing her, he waved it back and forth over her head. "You're the one who can read upside down."

"Is it a love letter?" Every time she reached for it, he pulled it away.

"Don't be silly." Pat drew the lamp closer. "It's from Joanna Pawlek." He glanced at the message written in a firm backhand script. "She says Mike Kulik has just had word that his wife is dead. She knows he's been friendly to us, and she thought we should know."

"I'm so sorry."

"Joanna says that he's taking it hard and is very depressed. She asked if I'd go and see him."

"You will, won't you?"

"Yes, I'll go." Pat asked, "Where's Mam?"

"At the Noonans'. The new baby is on the way and she's gone to help out."

"I want to talk to Cal—is he around?"

"He hasn't come home for supper yet. I stayed up to fix him something to eat but it's after ten now . . . he should have been here ages ago."

"He'll show up sooner or later. He always does."

"I know . . . but it's such a bad night." Annie went to the window and peered out. "I'm worried, Pat. I wonder where he could be."

❖ 8

It was unusual for his brother to be the first one out of bed in the morning. Pat dressed quickly and went down the stairs. His mother and sister were sitting together at the kitchen table, and they both seemed upset. "Where's Cal?"

"We don't know." Annie was ready to cry.

"He wasn't here when I came in late from the Noonans' last night." Mam looked exhausted. "I waited up but he never came home."

"Why didn't you wake me?"

"What good would that have done? You needed your rest, Pat. Besides . . . we know this has happened before."

They stared at each other. There had been fragrant evenings in late spring when Cal had stayed away from the house on secret missions of his own, hot nights in summer when he had disappeared over the mountain and arrived back a day or two later with a line of fish flapping slickly on a stick. His mother had scolded, his father had punished him out in the shed, but it had never stopped him from going again. Yet he had never vanished in March before, with the temperature down below freezing.

"I'll send word through the patch. You speak to the boys at the breaker. Surely someone will have seen him," Mam said, but she sounded frightened.

Before he left for work Pat went back up the stairs to search the attic room. Cal's favorite warm sweater, some underwear, and heavy socks appeared to be missing. On the old crate that they shared as a dresser, he was shocked to discover the glass pickle jar where he kept his hard-earned savings tipped over and emptied. It disturbed him to think that his brother had taken the money when Cal had never stolen anything before. He decided not to mention it to Mam.

"Hurry! You'll be late!" she called up from below.

As he left the house by the back door his feet went out from under him and he caught himself from falling just in time. A late-winter ice storm had come and gone in the night. Rooftops, sheds, and privies glistened, and each brittle twig of the pear tree was sheathed in pure glitter. The patch was a delicate world of glass, so fragile that to enter it smashed some of its fine brilliance. Pat felt a rush of delight. Cal, with his quick eye for wonder, would have whooped with joy and careened across the shining garden like a duck skidding down upon a frozen pond.

Anxious and withdrawn, he had cried in the night. Why? Except for a few trips to Freeland and one magical expedition to Hazleton for a Fourth of July parade, Cal had never been very far from home. Where had he gone?

Wavering, trying to keep his balance, Pat skidded along the slippery path. Farther on he met Ethel Dugan, who was always popping up at odd times in unlikely places with her nose running and her dirty petticoats dragging. Hands on her hips, she blocked his path.

"Pretty out, ain't it?"

"Yes, but move, Ethel. I'm in a hurry."

"You move." Arms flailing, feet skating away in all directions, she thrashed to stay upright. Impatient, Pat tried to maneuver around her, but instead they collided and crashed down together.

"You pushed me!" she shrieked.

"I did not!" He tried to rise, but she clawed at his trousers and he fell again, twisting an ankle. Pain shot up the side of his leg as he crawled to his knees and then struggled to get up.

"Too bad you didn't break your neck!" she bawled after him, and stuck out her tongue as he hobbled away.

Every time he tangled with Ethel bad luck was sure to follow.

The whistle blew before he reached Back Street. No one else was in sight. Hurting, out of breath, he saw loaded coal cars rolling up the track to the top of the breaker. By the time he reached the building the doors were locked and he pounded, hoping someone would let him slip in before the picker boss noticed his absence.

"You're late!" Blackie Pyle pushed him inside, swearing above the thump and rumble of the machinery.

"Only a few minutes . . . there was trouble at home."

"Don't give me no phony excuses. You'll be docked half a day's pay."

"That isn't fair!"

Pyle seized the front of Pat's coat, jerking him forward, so close their faces almost touched. "Get to work or get out for good . . . it's up to you!"

Pat wanted to strike out, hit the man with his fists, but all he could do was try to swallow his anger and obey. As he turned away he was kicked on the backside, so hard that he almost fell down. Chin up, he climbed the tiers through the billowing dust, knowing he would do what Cal had once done, sit on the bruises so Mam wouldn't see.

The only place he could find was beside Chester.

"Sit here, Flea . . . I won't bite you."

Ignoring him, Pat sat down and shoved his callused hands into the noisy black stream that poured toward him down the chute.

Joanna Pawlek had green tilted eyes, strong cheekbones, and blond hair that hung down her back in a thick gleaming braid. "I'm so glad you're here," she said as she opened the door.

Two little girls scarred with chicken pox were jumping on a rope bed in the corner, thumping each other with pillows, and gasping with laughter as feathers floated around the room.

"Stop that, Laura . . . you too, Sophie!" Joanna scooped up a plump crawling baby from the floor. "Come with me, Pat."

She stepped over a jumble of men's rubber boots and some scattered mining tools. "We have three boarders living with the seven of us, so you can see how crowded we are." Her face smiled back at him as she ducked under a clothesline strung with damp shirts and denim pants.

He followed her into the kitchen. The small room was roughly finished and insulated with newspapers. Strings of dried mushrooms hung on the wall near an ancient stove.

"Momma? This is my friend, Pat."

A barefoot woman, middle-aged and shapeless, was slapping dough around in circles on a table made from an old door. In spite of teeth missing in front, her smile was friendly and pleasant. "Pat? Yeah, I hear all about you! A real smart fella, eh? And you look good in the face just like she says."

The girl's smooth cheeks shone pink. "I asked him here because of Michael."

"That poor man is sad. Sick . . . in here"—Mrs. Pawlek tapped her forehead—"and in here." Solemnly she thumped her heavy breast. "He don't care no more about nothing. You go now and see."

"I'll take him up." Joanna kissed the baby's fuzzy golden head and handed her over to her mother. Halfway up the back staircase she stopped and took Pat's hand. "Momma saves her shoes to wear to church on Sunday," she whispered. "That way they don't wear out so fast."

"I didn't mean to stare . . . but how does she stand the cold?"

"We do what we must. It doesn't mean we are as ignorant as some people believe."

"I don't think that," Pat said. Had Alex told her he had shouted *stupid Polack* at Chester?

"I know you don't. You've always been kinder than the other boys, Pat. It's why I've always looked up to you."

She was still an inch or two taller. What she meant was that since the first day she started school in Scatter Patch, a sturdy glowing child of ten with only a few words of English, he was the one she had picked out to admire. She had sat next to him in class, watched him play ball during recess, and followed him home at a respectful distance. Guiltily, Pat wondered why she should think so well of him when he had usually ignored her, pretending she didn't exist.

Standing close to her in the narrow space he felt strange mixed emotions, the old need to escape and a heady new one, a wish to stay close to her in the tingling darkness with her breath falling warm against his face and her fingers curled tight around his.

She turned and went up the rest of the way. A lamp burned unsteadily in the shadowy loft. The small space was crowded with the boarders' possessions. Three ticks stuffed with leaves were spread upon the floor, and on one of them a man lay with a ragged quilt drawn up to his unshaven chin.

"Michael," Joanna called softly. "Someone is here to see you."

Kulik stirred under the covers and then raised himself slightly.

"I came to tell you how sorry we are . . . about your wife." Pat didn't know what else to say.

"Thank you." The miner sank down again upon the mattress. After a long pause he said, "Two years ago when I left Poland I promised I would send for her soon. It took longer to save money than I thought it would. The agents who brought us here told so many lies." He spoke slowly and with difficulty, as if it took too much energy to express his heavy thoughts. "Now Elizabeth is dead and I have nothing."

"You have friends here."

"I have *nothing*," the man repeated bitterly. "We are not welcome in this country. People laugh and make jokes about us, call us bad names. It is very hard. We came without money, but we brought our music and stories and a thousand years of memories; yet these rich things mean nothing in this poor unhappy place."

There was silence in the gloomy attic room.

"Please, Michael," Joanna said. "Won't you come downstairs and have something to eat? You could play with the baby a little . . ."

He shook his head, turning his sad face away from the flickering lamplight.

"Is there anything we can do?" Pat remembered how often Mike had come to his house after his father had died, and never empty-handed.

"Nothing," Mike whispered. "Nothing."

"Even with all of us here he seems so alone. I thought it might help him to know that others cared," Joanna said. In the front room Sophie and Laura were hiding under the fat feather pillows, the rope bed shaking with their laughter. "He's not eating . . . and he hasn't been to work in days."

"What will happen to him?"

"He'll probably go back to Poland. And we'll miss him. Michael is such a good person . . . he is like one of our family."

At the door, Pat told her about Cal and asked her to let him know if she heard any news.

"I'll speak to the men when they come from the saloon tonight. But he could have headed west, you know . . . like so many others."

"He wouldn't do that."

"I've seen him walking around looking miserable. I think he hated it here. Who could blame him?"

"I know he'll be back."

"I'm sorry about this." Joanna's warm hand touched Pat's arm. "I hope you hear something soon."

On his way home he passed men coming from Gogarty's tavern, smelled the lager on their breath, and caught bits of excited conversation.

"They may be high and mighty now but we'll bend 'em . . . we'll bend 'em." It was the low, whispery voice of Mr. Daly, whose lungs were ruined, and who sometimes left a trail of red drops splashed after him in the snow. The old contract was almost up, but company officials still refused to consider a new one. Recently, union organizers had spread through the patch, hoping to sign up new members. Early in the morning and late at night they stood at the pit head or in vacant lots or on street corners to pass out information, answer questions, and give speeches. They weren't there to curse the mine owners, most of them said, but to compel them to give miners the right to bargain for their own labor. *Collective bargaining* was the term they used.

Everywhere men were speaking more openly about their grievances.

Pat thought of his father, who had seldom talked about his troubles. Cal was like that, too. Where was he and why had he gone? All day Pat had worried about him, but now he was angry. With three of them working it had been hard enough to manage, but what would they do if Cal didn't come back?

He didn't want to think about that—or believe what Joanna had said.

❖ 9

Old Father Reilly had had a stroke and been replaced by a younger man from Mauch Chunk. Father Conlin rose several inches over six feet and possessed a big radish nose that glowed an even brighter red when he was excited over something, which was most of the time.

Annie was one of the first to talk to him after his arrival at the end of March. She had been on an errand for Mrs. Eliot when she saw the new priest unloading his belongings and helped him carry them into the rectory.

"He says he was born in a coal patch, too," she reported to her family later in the evening. "He worked in the mines himself when he was a boy, and that's why he believes in trade unions. He even knows John Mitchell personally! I asked him if he had ever met Mother Jones and he hadn't, but he told me all about her. She lost her husband and four children in a yellow fever epidemic years ago, and she's been involved in the labor movement ever since. He called her a holy terror, but he smiled when he said it."

Annie was fascinated by what she had read about the tiny, elderly lady who had charged through the anthracite region during a strike two years earlier, haranguing men to join the United Mine Workers. Sweet-faced, rough-spoken, and fearless, she had a special empathy for miners; and it tickled Annie that she was sometimes described as the most dangerous woman in America.

"Father Conlin has piles of books," she went on. "Not all of them are boring religious ones, either. He told me I may borrow any of the novels he considers fit."

"He doesn't know it's only the *unfit* ones you'll want to read." Pat grinned.

Annie laughed. "He adores baseball. He wants to organize some teams here in the spring."

"I can't believe you just stood by and listened to this man tell you the story of his entire life," Mam said. "I'm sure you had something to say."

"Yes, quite a lot," Annie admitted. "I told him what happened to Dad and about Cal leaving and how we haven't heard one single word, and he was very sorry about it. Then I told him how glad I was Father Reilly was gone because he was so mean and bad-tempered and cuffed the altar boys and always gave me twice as much penance as Brigit Noonan and you know what a liar she is. I also said that Mr. Eliot might lock up the school at night because he's heard that Brian Foley is giving the miners uppity ideas."

"You'd better hope that HIS MAJESTY doesn't find out which way your tongue is wagging," Mam warned, "or he'll send you packing in a hurry."

"Everyone is too worried about Peter to pay any attention to me. They didn't even notice how long I was gone this afternoon."

"What's the matter with him?" Pat felt guilty. He had avoided Peter ever since the night he had gone to see the piano.

"He's sick again, but you know how he's always ailing. This time it's a terrible big cough and high fever. Dr. Argy came again today."

Pat thought about Peter on the way to class. He had his faults, but he was fun to be with and he had plenty of courage. Once they had explored an abandoned mine shaft together, ignoring the DANGER sign, hearing the stealthy plink of water and rats skittering through the sour darkness, feeling the slimy walls squeezing in as the tunnel grew smaller. Pat had been the first to turn back.

He had been upset the night Mrs. Eliot had sent him away, but it hadn't been Peter's fault. He would ask Annie to tell Peter that he hoped he would soon be well again.

Many of the younger boys had dropped out of night school when they discovered it wasn't going to be a social event, a warm place for a good time on a cold winter evening. Most of them were too tired after a long day in the breaker to concentrate on the textbooks. Cezlak was the first to leave, then Kenny Bowen, Francis Shanahan, and Will O'Neill. Now only a few remained. Alex Pawlek was a serious student and Kevin Dugan, in spite of his giggling fits and love of fun, had a quick, curious mind.

"You'll go if I have to drag you there," Mam threatened, but that wasn't the reason Pat stayed. He secretly admired the schoolmaster. Self-taught, Foley was a natural teacher and his dark eyes burned with his need to communicate all he knew. Each night he roamed the aisles, stopping here and there to listen as his pupils pushed their fingers slowly across the pages of the readers, stumbling out words.

"You couldn't function in a mine without a carbide lamp," he had told them from the start. "Literacy is a light that will show you shining worlds that you never knew existed."

It was only after they had wrestled with reading and arithmetic and grammar and the texts were closed that he spoke informally of other things: government, economics, and politics, sometimes poetry or literature, music or art. Even though they were free to leave, almost everyone stayed. No one slept or talked or chewed tobacco; the only sounds were the teacher's deep voice, the frequent coughing, and the distant howl of a train flying by in the night.

For the first time, Pat had a shadowy grasp of the great sprawling life beyond the slag heaps and felt some connection to the rest of the country. And he noticed how Foley almost always concluded with the subject that interested him most, the welfare of miners.

"Did you know that since 1842 men in this region have been demanding safer working conditions and better pay? Then why have they failed *time* after *time* after *time*?

"The Workmen's Benevolent Association, the Knights of Labor, and other organizations tried and failed . . . not because they were radical—the truth is that most miners oppose strikes and violence—but because men in the Northern and Middle and Southern fields weren't able to unify to achieve a common goal. And, because they stayed divided, our history is one of beatings and bloodshed and *failure* after *failure* after *failure*."

He was slapping books down on the desk, getting ready for dismissal, leaving them with one last comment.

"The acceptance of trade unions is only now coming of age in this country. One day, employers will be forced to admit that laborers have a right to a living wage, a right to be protected in the workplace and some compensation for injury or death."

What he was trying to do, Pat sensed, was to give the tired men in the classroom some knowledge of the past and a hope for the future. But not everyone was impressed with his fine talk. A crudely printed poster saying STAY HOME SOCIALIST SCUM had been nailed to his door and a shot was fired over his head one night as he walked home in the dark.

Pat thought he knew why. What Foley was also giving them, both the native and the foreign-born, was a feeling of self-worth and pride in what they contributed. But if they valued themselves, then they would be harder to control; obviously that dangerous possibility would worry company officials.

"Do you really think there'll be a strike?" Pat was walking home after class with Alex and Kevin. He and Alex were friendly again and had been working together at the breaker.

"I hope not." Kevin shivered in his thin jacket; the Dugans

never had warm clothing to wear. "The last time my father stayed at home he beat us up all the time. I was black-and-blue for weeks."

They were in Cork Lane, crowded three abreast. As they approached the Noonan house Pat heard the usual shrieks and screams, something smashed against a wall, a back door slamming shut.

"If there is one," Alex said, "I hope nothing terrible happens. My Uncle Andrew was killed at the massacre at Lattimer in 'ninety-seven."

"Killed! How?" Pat asked.

"It started at Honeybrook Colliery over at McAdoo, where my cousin Joseph was a driver . . . he was about fifteen then." Alex stopped, pulled a stub of cigarette from his pocket, and fumbled for a match. "They had a new superintendent there called Gomer Jones. He ordered the drivers to return the mules to the stables at the end of the day and take care of them . . . but without extra pay." Light from a match winked briefly in the darkness. "They got so mad that he kicked them out, so then the miners went on strike. Jones picked up a crowbar and attacked one of them and almost got his head busted in. He was lucky to stay alive." Slowly Alex inhaled, then passed the cigarette on to Kevin. "The union was just getting started around here and men were marching from place to place trying to sign up new members. There was so much trouble that all the mines closed down, except over at Lattimer. But the fellas there let it be known that if others came and asked them to go out on strike, then they would."

They were standing in front of Pat's house, and when

Kevin offered him the smoldering butt he took a quick nervous puff, hoping his mother wasn't looking out the window. She had eyes like a cat.

"Most of the strikers were immigrants like my people," Alex went on. "From Poland and Lithuania and Hungary ... and at first they were afraid, see? They remembered how it was in the Old Country."

"Yeah ... speak up and get shot, right?" Kevin laughed.

"Yes, but they were told it was different here, that they had a *right* to protest, as long as there wasn't any violence. You know, like all that freedom stuff that Foley pounds into us."

"But it's true, isn't it?" Pat said.

"Well, they must have believed it, because about four hundred of them decided to march to Lattimer with nothing to protect them except an American flag. Sheriff Martin in Hazleton was expecting trouble, so he rounded up a posse ... all respectable businessmen, of course." Alex's slow calm voice was bitter. "They met the strikers walking through the west part of the city and tried to stop them, but the miners said they weren't breaking any laws and the mayor backed them up. Naturally the sheriff didn't like it when they kept on going."

"So what did he do about it?" Kevin's teeth were rattling in the cold, and he wanted to speed Alex up.

"He and the posse took the streetcar and got to Lattimer first. When the mob came into sight they opened fire. That's when my uncle was killed, along with eighteen others. Thirty-nine more were badly hurt ... some were crippled for life. There was a trial later on, but the sheriff and the posse all got off."

"What happened to your cousin?" Pat asked.

"Joseph was there that day and saw it all, but luckily he wasn't hurt. He was the one who told me what happened. So no matter what Foley says about American justice, my people had to learn something all over again: Speak up and get shot!"

◆ 10

Spring prowled closer, rubbing its soft green flanks against the mountains, pawing under pockets of crumbling snow to uncover the first chaste blossoms of trailing arbutus. Soon pink and white dogwood would flower, then honeysuckle and laurel and sweet-scented wild roses.

Every year, from a high secluded lookout, Pat noticed more dark patches gashing the surrounding hills. These were the strippings, raw abrasions where coal was blasted loose and scraped from the surface. Here April glided by at a distance, skirting the shattered birches and the rusty foliage.

One Sunday after church he leaned against a sunwarmed rock and stared out across the valley. It felt good to be alone and away from the house. It had been difficult ever since Cal had gone, weeks ago; they had waited for news, worrying and wondering, but no word had come and Mam had taken it hard. Her husband had died, her oldest son had disappeared, and Michael Kulik, who had taken a friendly interest and had been helpful to her, had left the patch without saying good-bye. Now all her anger, hurt, and frustration were focused on Pat, and it didn't seem fair. All he did was go to work and to night school; yet she was suspicious when he was out of her sight and quarrelsome with him when he was at home.

Rumors of a strike coming soon meant there could be even rougher times ahead. Pat knew they couldn't exist on Annie's tiny wages if the breaker shut down.

Hearing the rustle of branches, the crackle of twigs snapping underfoot, he waited to see who had discovered the almost hidden path. Moments later a girl burst out of the shrubbery, pink-faced and breathless from the steep uphill climb. She stopped in surprise, stared, and then laughed. "Pat! What are you doing here?"

Joanna was warm and perspiring. She had pushed up the sleeves of her blue cotton dress, exposing her strong, rounded arms. Moisture trickled down her flushed cheeks and beaded her curved upper lip.

"I come here whenever I can. How did you find this place?"

She laughed again. "You think I followed you, don't you? That's silly . . . I'm not a little girl anymore."

Her bright hair, freed from the tight restraining braid, had a wild, leaping life of its own. Pat had a strange impulse to tug it smooth in his hands.

"I've been here lots of times." Joanna shaded her eyes, looking far into the distance. "It's so still and peaceful, and I never have a quiet minute at home." She showed him the parcel she had with her. "I brought a lunch . . . would you like some?"

"No, thanks." He felt shy about sharing her food.

"Well, I'm always hungry!" She sat down on a patch of sun-splashed ground and brought out some dark bread and hard cheese. "Did you know I'd left school?"

"Alex told me you were working at the squib factory."

Many young girls made fuses for the explosives used in mining operations in a rundown place on the road that led to Freeland.

"Well, I hate it. It's horrible and filthy, but worst of all, it's boring. It's awful waking up in the morning knowing what I'll be doing every minute for the rest of the day. That's why I like to come here to make my plans."

"What plans?"

"Someday," she said, "I'm going to get on a train and travel all the way to California."

"Why?"

"Why do you think? For the adventure, of course! *California*," she repeated. "Isn't that the most wonderful name? It makes me think of fresh air and sunshine and an ocean that's as clean as soapsuds. And I just can't wait to get there!"

She had taken a tremendous leap beyond him. Pat knew no ordinary Pennsylvania girl would have dreamed up such an impossible scheme. "What's your hurry?"

"For one thing, my father wants to get me off his hands. I swear he'd have tried to marry me off if Michael hadn't gone away."

The idea shocked Pat. "Joanna . . . you're too young!"

"I'm fifteen now . . . that's grown."

"Things aren't done that way here."

"Poppa's head is still in Poland. He thinks he's looking out for me, but I can look after myself. If I ever do get married I'll pick out a man of my own—someone a few thousand miles from here."

Everything she said in her fresh, confident voice surprised Pat and, for some reason, annoyed him. "It would cost too much to go that far."

"That's why I've started saving now. A few pennies put away every week will soon add up."

He wanted to bring her down to earth. "What if there's a strike and the factory closes down?"

"Do you think it will happen?"

"It looks that way ... maybe soon."

"Then it will just take longer." The green eyes lifted coolly. "You don't believe I can do it, do you? Well, I'm not going to sit on a slag heap the rest of my life. I can do as I please."

"Only rich people do that."

"Then I'll *get* rich."

He laughed at her. "How?"

"I sew well enough. I'll open a dress shop in San Francisco and make plenty of money. I *am* going someday ... just like Cal." She got to her feet and came toward him, bright sparks of sunlight flashing in her hair. "One of the boarders told me something that you ought to know ... I can't get it out of my mind. In the mine ... where Cal sat by the door ... he drew birds on the wall with white chalk."

"He was just passing time."

"But maybe it means something, Pat. Think of it ... hundreds and hundreds of lovely white birds, all flying up in the darkness."

Flying away. Was that what Cal wanted to do? For the first

time Pat faced the fact that his brother might not be coming back.

There was a problem with the rollers, and the breaker was forced to shut down on the following Saturday. As boys rushed joyfully from the building, Boomer Gogarty invited them to a cockfight he was promoting behind the tavern later in the day. These were always popular events in the patch, but Pat had gone once and seen two handsome birds savagely peck each other to bloody tatters, and he never wanted to do it again.

He was glad to have time off. The picker boss made life miserable for him now, screaming at him that his work was sloppy, slashing at him with his stick. He'd learned to keep his mouth shut, but he still saw ways in which things could be improved. There were so many injuries, so much illness. Recently Shanahan had cut his hand badly, blood poisoning had set in, and he had been sent to the miner's hospital at Drifton to recover. Jimmie Reese's bronchitis was so bad from breathing in dust that he was forced to stay at home, and his mother was moaning to everyone about his lost wages.

Pat thought he would go up the mountain again if he could manage to slip away before his mother found some chores for him to do. She was always so irritable now, her nerves rubbed raw, she said, from trying to feed them on so little money. At least Annie got a square meal at the Eliots' every day. He wished he did.

Cutting across lots, taking a short cut home, Pat saw Ethel in her ragtag clothing and ugly brown tam, aimlessly kicking a can along Scotch Row. When she saw him she pulled at a metal chain around her neck and waggled a mangy rabbit's foot in his direction.

Nothing had gone right since she had won it from him months ago. If only he could get it back he was sure his luck would change.

Annie was alone at home staring out the window.

"Why aren't you over at the Eliots?" he asked her.

She turned to him, her face red and wrinkled from crying. "Pat! I'm so glad that you're here . . . you have to help me!"

"What's the matter?"

"Nobody told me what to do this morning. You know that Peter's been sick for a while, and the doctor was there again . . . I just kept getting in the way. So I slipped into the parlor for a quick look at the paper. I only wanted to see if there was anything written up about a strike coming."

"Never mind the strike, Annie. Just tell me what happened."

"Mrs. Eliot must have needed me. Anyway, she came looking, and when she caught me reading *The Inquirer* you should have heard the awful things she said. She told me Mr. Smythe had warned her about me and said I was insolent and I'm *not*, Pat . . . you know I'm not! Then she screamed at me to leave!"

"*You've been let go?*"

Annie nodded.

"Maybe it's not as bad as you think. Maybe she'll change her mind."

"No, she won't. She meant every word. She's glad to get rid of me."

Pat tried to stay calm, think clearly. "Peter told me he'd speak up for you if there was trouble. I'm sure he'll ask his mother to keep you on."

Annie was crying again. "But I hate it there! I don't want to stay on!"

Pat wanted to scold her and then he just felt sorry. "Don't you understand that you have to go back? Cal's gone, maybe for good. If there's a strike I'll be out of a job, and we'll all be depending on you."

"On *me?*" Annie swallowed, wiping her shocked, wet face with her hands. She looked childish and frightened. "Then you'd better go and ask Peter to help. Do it now, before Mam comes home."

"Where is she?"

"Over at the Noonans' steaming young Georgie. He has the croup, and Brigit came hollering for help just as I got in the door. Mam doesn't know why I was early, and I don't want her to find out!"

When he reached The Palace, Pat stood in the street trying to find enough nerve to open the gate. Finally he did it, wondering what he would do if Mrs. Eliot refused to let him see Peter.

No one answered his knock. He rapped again, louder this time, his heart jumping fast in his chest. There were heavy, dragging footsteps within, and the door opened slowly. The tall, thin woman standing in the entrance had a dazed empty expression, and Pat didn't think she recognized him. Quickly he said what he had come to say. "I'm a friend of Peter's, Mrs.

Eliot. I was here once before, but I guess you don't remember me."

A deep voice from inside asked, "Who is it, Leah?"

"Nobody," she answered vaguely. "Just some boy."

Pat continued in a rush. "Could I see him, please . . . just for a minute? I know he's not well, but this is very important."

"You want to speak to my boy?"

He nodded.

"Peter is gone." Her voice was so low that he wasn't sure he had heard her correctly.

"But where did he go?"

The door closed. Puzzled, he waited on the porch, trying to decide what to do. A few minutes later Dr. Argy came out of the house carrying a familiar black bag. His face was grave as he put a hand on Pat's shoulder. "I'm sorry, son. I know how hard it is to lose a friend."

Confused, Pat stared at him in silence.

"Mrs. Eliot didn't tell you?" The doctor was startled. "Poor soul, I'm not sure she's grasped it yet herself."

Then he brushed past and hurried away.

• 11

S*trike!* For weeks the dangerous word had rustled through the Pennsylvania coal fields.

Strike! Strike! A movement coiled like a serpent and ready to rise.

Strike! Strike! Strike! Swift, lunging release as one hundred forty-five thousand men in the anthracite region poured out of the mines and into the streets. Stooped, gaunt, and sallow, they stood idle and uneasy, eyes squinting in the clear, bright light of early May.

"Let's go! Let's go!" Machinery screeched to a halt; sturdy lokies, loaded with coal, stood still on the tracks as six thousand young slate pickers streamed away from the dark, dusty breakers, whooping at the pleasure of running free, out of doors.

The president of the mine workers' union believed that strikes were a last, desperate measure, almost an act of war. He had hoped to prevent a walkout, but when the company owners refused to negotiate a new contract, delegates at the UMW convention in Hazleton had voted for it.

"All right, then," John Mitchell said, giving his support. "If you stand as one man, you will win. Divide and you will lose."

In Scatter Patch, women talked with other women at communal hydrants and across weathered gray fences. Even the smaller children felt an electric tension in the air and sensed a dark event hovering over them like a threatening storm. During the first emotional moments, an effigy of Mr. Eliot was strung up and burned, and nonunion miners were jeered at and stoned. Gangs of rowdy youths ran through the lanes, shouting and swearing, and setting off firecrackers that crackled like bullets. At night, men set fires on company property, to mine sheds and timber, but as union organizers spread through the region, urging people to stay calm and controlled, the first angry reaction sputtered out.

"The president of the Lackawanna Railroad said he was sure there wouldn't be a strike because he didn't think the men had any grievances." Annie's light-blue eyes swiftly scanned the newspapers scattered around her on the kitchen table, eager for every detail. In a mocking voice she read, "'After our men have been idle for a while with their families to support, and no wages coming in, they may take a different view of the strike. We are confident that they will regret their action, and be glad to resume work on the old terms.'"

"I don't think so," Pat said. "Not this time."

"It really *is* like war, isn't it? Except it's a battle of wills . . . and thank goodness there aren't any bombs going off."

"Not yet . . . and I hope it doesn't come to that," Pat said, but both of them knew that people had been murdered during strikes.

"Haven't you started that washing yet, girl?" Mam called from the front room, where she had begun a vigorous spring cleaning. She had been more hot-tempered and bossier than usual since Annie had been dismissed from the Eliots'. "I never wanted you to go there in the first place," she'd fumed after it happened, "but I never expected you'd be sent away like a criminal. And to think that Brigit Noonan is over there dusting the china instead."

"I'll get the water for you." Pat collected the pails from the shed, glad to escape from the house.

On his way to the ballpark, later in the afternoon, he heard the uproar inside the saloon and slipped inside to listen in on the conversation. Most of the men there were noisy and talkative, elated at having taken a defiant stand.

"A fair day's wage for a fair day's work," Mr. Pawlek roared out as he sat with his Polish friends in the hazy, smoke-filled room. "That's what we want and we'll stay out until we get it."

"I want something else." Mr. Daly, thin and shrunken, spoke from the end of the bar. "I want those big guns to see us as more than a mob of blackened faces that all look alike." He coughed and took a long swallow of beer. "I'd like them to know that we have power, too . . . and to respect it."

"Respect?" Mr. Noonan, flushed and unsteady, signaled Mr. Gogarty to splash more whiskey into his glass from a bottle of Old Overholt. "It'll snow in hell before we get any of that." He was a mild, cheerful man who always emerged from his stormy household wildly mussed, as if he'd been blown out in a gale. "So I'll take whatever loose change we can jingle out of them laddy bucks and not expect miracles." His watery glance wavered in Pat's direction and he beckoned him over. "It's time you had a drink, son. Let me buy you one to wet your whistle."

Pat wanted to accept, to feel he was part of the rebellious movement, but he quickly refused and ducked out of the place, knowing his mother would skin him alive if she knew where he'd been. THAT DISGRACE was what she called the tavern. It was their liking for alcohol that was the sad, dark side of the Irish, she'd warned him. "Oh, they've a wonderful light touch with the joking and music and a magic gift of gab, for sure ... but they can't handle their liquor. Darcy took the pledge on the day we were married and he never went back on his word. *Don't You Start!*"

Honey Callahan's troubles had come about because of his fondness for the hard stuff, she said. "And you're his spitting image!" Sometimes Pat caught her gazing at him in a peculiar way, as if she suspected he might have inherited some of his grandfather's unlucky tendencies. Did she really expect him to end up in jail?

Every day more men were leaving the patch, hoping to find work in the cities or in the soft coal fields of Appalachia.

"I could go, too," Pat said. "Try and find a job somewhere else. I might even meet up with Cal."

"That's ridiculous." Any mention of the missing boy greatly agitated Mam. "Not one word from him in all this time ...

there's no telling where he might be. He might be dead for all we know."

It was what Pat now secretly feared.

"No, you'll stay here with Annie and me," Mam decided. "The strike might be over any day."

He didn't tell her how unlikely that was, but he did mention how many of the immigrant laborers had left Gruber's Hotel and gone away on "Johnny Mitchell specials." These were the freight trains that carried them to New York, where they waited for passage back to their homelands.

"Good riddance to bad rubbish," Mam snapped. "They had their nerve coming here in the first place, stealing jobs away from decent Americans."

"It wasn't like that." Lately everything his mother said got on Pat's nerves. "Mr. Foley told us that agents were sent over to Europe to sign on as many men as they could at low wages. So don't blame the foreigners."

"But I do. They're nothing but troublemakers, and this strike is all their fault."

"That isn't true. Don't you understand that union members voted and a majority decided it?"

"What I do understand is that BIG SHOTS with money have always told people without it what to do, and nothing will ever change that."

"Mr. Foley thinks trade unions will."

"He's to blame, too. Stirring up ignorant men with his socialist drivel!"

She was upset, unreasonable, unfair. It was what happened during strikes; people were frightened, frustrated; emotions boiled over, often into violence. Already barbed wire bristled throughout the region, and armed guards were on patrol. Stay away from company property, union officials warned the residents of the coal communities. *Don't provoke the Coal & Iron police. Operators want the outside world to believe that strikers are dangerous, in order to get public opinion on their side.*

By the middle of June, Scatter Patch seemed quiet and empty. The fruit huckster's plaintive "bananios . . . bananios . . ." was no longer heard along the crooked lanes, and the scissors grinder and fish peddler failed to appear. Every day Mr. Gogarty stood glumly at the door of the tavern, hoping for customers, but there were few who could afford a mug of chilled lager.

Night classes had been suspended shortly before the strike when Mr. Eliot, who had been told that Brian Foley was spreading radical notions among the men, had angrily ordered that the schoolhouse be locked in the evenings. On the following Sunday Father Conlin had told his parishioners, "When this trouble is over, Mr. Foley will continue his excellent instruction in the parish hall." His words had been reported to the superintendent, and after that he, too, was viewed with alarm and suspicion by company management. Pat didn't miss the homework, but he did miss the exciting discussions that had taken place, the men shouting out questions and the teacher pacing back and forth across the room, singing out answers.

He still wakened at six every morning. The habit of getting up early was difficult to break. Full of restless energy, he scrubbed floors and washed windows, wiping the glass with newspaper to make it sparkle. He tried to make small repairs around the house, fix things that his mother nagged him about, but he could never please her. "I wish you had Cal's knack for carpentry," she complained.

When he replaced the broken shingles on the roof, careful not to walk under the ladder, Annie laughed at him. "How can you believe such silly, superstitious stuff?"

"My father was the very same," Mam said in a dark, knowing way. "He'd never dare throw a hat on the bed, and he'd a mortal dread of the number thirteen. Oh, isn't it queer how much you're like him, Pat!" And the boy felt Honey Callahan's ghost peering over his shoulder again.

He had already spaded the yard and planted a garden. Growing produce was very important; cabbages usually lasted until after Christmas, and potatoes, stored under sand in the cellar, until the following spring. This year his mother insisted that he use every available inch of soil for the vegetables, but he put in a narrow border of flowers for her anyway, figuring they were a kind of nourishment as well. "We can't eat petunias and snapdragons!" was all that she said.

He spent long, hot hours crouching among the ruffled rows, weeding lettuce, carrots, and radishes, beets, beans, and onions. Meals had been so meager for so long that he now looked forward to fresh salad greens after pale months without them. Later there would be turnips and cauliflower, squash and melons, pumpkins for the Thanksgiving pies.

The best part of the day was when he put away the garden tools and headed for ball practice. Father Conlin had organized two teams: Pat and his friends, called the Breakers, met at a rough park on the far side of the village, while the immigrant boys, named Lokies after the railroad cars that transported the coal, played on a cindery patch beyond Back Street.

Every afternoon Pat felt the same flash of raw pleasure as his ragged glove sucked in a high ball or his clean new bat stroked a hit far into center field. A home run always stretched him six feet tall. Often the games went on for hours, ending only after dark.

The priest had arranged for the Breakers to play against the Lokies as a main event on the Fourth of July, and Pat couldn't wait. Chester Cezlak was the best man on the Lokies' team, and Pat dreamed of beating him in a contest where size didn't count much, where it was skill and confidence that mattered most.

"I don't remember." Annie's small face was pinched with guilt and fear. "I was reading in the privy, and when I left the yard later on I don't know whether I shut the gate or not."

"It could have been me," Pat said. "I was in a hurry to go and play ball," but he was almost certain that his sister, dreamy and forgetful, was at fault. How could she have been so careless!

"It doesn't matter . . . the damage is done." Mam stared at the mangled garden, where tender, growing vegetables had been trampled and destroyed. Slowly she seemed to swell and glow with anger. "I will strangle that goat!" She raised her deep voice to a shout. "STRANGLE IT AND BOIL IT UP FOR SOUP!"

Silence at the Noonan house, across the lane. No slamming doors or sobbing children, not a yip out of Yap, not a sign of Old Sport. Pat had a sense of everyone's lying low until the storm blew over. "Not everything's ruined ... what's under the ground is all right. There's still time to plant again," he said, but the idea depressed him.

His mother refused to be comforted. "It's a catastrophe," she whispered. "We're going to have to ask for help and I can't—I won't ... I'd rather starve."

There had been bad times before, some worse than others, but Pat knew his father had always managed to put food on the table. Now it was *his* responsibility to provide, and he didn't know how he would do it.

It was an empty time of hunger, a succession of bitter days when he felt as if his stomach had twisted inside out. They ate mush until the cornmeal ran out and after that, boiled greens. Every time he saw Old Sport cavorting through the patch, Pat imagined him roasted on a platter, with an apple in his mouth. Some mornings, when he wakened, he thought he smelled fresh bread in the oven, but when he went down the stairs he found the kitchen range was cold; there was no sense in boiling a kettle with no tea in the cupboard. Mam and Annie went searching for the tiny wild strawberries that were ripening sweet and red upon the hills, but no matter how many they brought home he could never feel satisfied.

He went into the woods with his slingshot, desperately trying to get a rabbit or a squirrel and missing every chance; twice he walked the long distance over the mountain to fish in the lake where his brother had always had luck, but both times he came back empty-handed. Ashamed, he raged silently, *Where are you ... why aren't you here when we need you,* even though his fears about Cal grew bigger and colder every day.

His fifteenth birthday arrived without fanfare, not that he had expected anything under the circumstances. Annie made him a card and gave him a warm hug, but his mother only said, "I hope you weren't expecting a cake," and was quiet and preoccupied all morning. "I'm going to ask Father Conlin for a handout," she announced finally, looking tense but resolved. "I won't see you two suffer any longer. There's no other way, but it shames me, it does."

"Yes, there is," Pat said. "Let me leave . . . I'll find work somewhere else."

"No!" Fiercely, Mam pinned on her hat with a long, shining pin. "I don't want you to go."

"This strike might drag on for months." His voice cracked with frustration. "I have to find something to do . . . some way to help out."

"Mam!" Returning from the post office, Annie ran into the house. "It's for you!" She pointed to words crudely scrawled across the envelope she held in her hand. "It must be from Cal!"

Quickly her mother took it, tore it open, and shook out some bills. "Five dollars!" Then her face sagged with disappointment. "But there isn't any message . . . not even a return address."

Happy and relieved, Pat glanced at the postmark. "This was mailed from Pittston . . . that's only twenty miles away!"

"Then maybe he'll be home for the holiday." Annie was bouncing with excitement.

"No . . . he wouldn't have sent this if he were planning to

come." Mam clutched the money tightly. "Still, he's thinking about us and looking out for us . . . this will tide us over for a little while." Impulsively she flung her arms around them. "Oh, I knew he wouldn't let us down. And thank goodness he's *safe!*"

Pat hugged her back. Even if they didn't know where Cal was living or what he was doing, the awful strain of worry was over at last, and he couldn't have had a better birthday gift than that.

Everyone in Scatter Patch looked forward to the Fourth of July, celebrated every year with booming speeches, picnics, and outdoor games and exploding in a golden burst of fireworks at the end. Pat had never imagined anything finer until his family had traveled on a special miners' excursion train to Hazleton when he was twelve.

That was the first time he had seen the busy city, starred and striped with wind-whipped flags, or watched a glittering parade flow past on Broad Street.

"Look . . . *look!*" Annie had been beside herself at the sight of so many colorful floats, at firemen riding the sparkling red engines, at carriages shining with dignitaries, all of them bowing like royalty. "Oh, *listen!*" She had loved the spine-bumping shudder of drums, the brassy, clapping smash of cymbals, as the marching bands stepped briskly by.

After it was over they had explored the bustling streets, gaped at a piano factory and a brewery, admired shops and crowded restaurants.

"I wish we could eat in one of those fancy places," Annie

said. "I'd order oysters and caviar and French champagne." She had read how millionaires in New York served such elegant things at their lavish banquets and costume parties.

Instead they ate a picnic lunch in a pleasant green park.

Later, as they strolled by the handsome big houses around the square, Mam had stopped to admire a mansion draped with patriotic bunting. "Glory be . . . how grand. Just look at all those shiny windows. It reminds me of Philadelphia."

Annie was wistful. "Living here must be like a holiday that never ends."

"I wish this one would." Smiling, her father had given her hand a squeeze. "All this walking hurts my feet."

The boys were too awed by the sights to talk much. Going home at night had been like returning to a tiny distant country where the landscape was dim and the climate was gray. The trip to Hazleton had glowed in Pat's mind for days. Then the dust that sifted into every crack and cranny of the coal patch seemed to drift over the memory, clouding all the bright images.

◆ 12

Every male left in the coal patch, every big, little, and in-between child, streamed toward the ballpark in the shimmering afternoon. Women went, too, with babies in their arms and younger ones following hand-in-hand, everyone pleased at having somewhere to go, something to cheer about at last.

Grimly the Coal & Iron police patrolled company property, revolvers at their hips, a surly guard dog panting at their heels.

Pat went with his mother and sister, wishing Cal and his father could have been there, too. Maybe if he had been able to walk with the men of the family he would have felt less nervous and unsure of himself. Yet he was proud of how nice the McFarlane women looked in their starched white shirt-waists and dark neat skirts. Annie's cheeks were as pink as the fragrant wild roses she had pinned to the brim of her hat.

Ahead of them, the Noonan family paraded along the dusty lane, husband and wife linked arm-in-arm with Brigit tugging a long kite of children behind, and Old Sport frisking along at the rear.

A large crowd had gathered at the playing field, where people laughed and chatted with their friends. Some of the miners who had found work on farms in the valley were home for the day. Pat, aware of how many different languages were spoken on an occasion meant to celebrate national unity, thought there was something odd and disturbing in that.

"There's Father Conlin!" Annie laughed as the tall, lanky figure paced restlessly, waiting for the game to begin. "Nobody can say a Holy Roman Umpire won't be fair."

"You can be sure there'll be some who will even dispute the word of a priest." Mam glanced severely at some Methodist women standing nearby, but then her attention was caught by someone waving a baby's tiny fist in their direction. "Son? Isn't that the Polish girl who used to follow you home from school?"

"Yes, but she's different now." Pat watched Joanna hand the infant over to her mother and then dash toward them, the prim braid gone for good, her bright unruly hair flying loose around her animated face.

"I'm so excited—aren't you?" She had a wide, happy smile for all of them. "Of course, I'll be yelling for both teams to win, but I just had to come and wish you luck, Pat." She squeezed his arm, slipped something into his pocket, and then ran back to rejoin her family.

"Different?" Mam's mouth was crimped with disapproval. "Why, she's still as bold as brass . . . and a great ungainly thing as well."

"I think she's beautiful," Annie insisted. "And clever, too. But this place is too small for Joanna. She has such wonderful *big* plans."

"Does she now." Mam looked doubtful. "I just hope your brother isn't part of them."

"I'll see you after the game." As Pat crossed the diamond he thought over what Annie had said. *Joanna has such wonderful big plans.* Mam needn't worry, then. There was no room in his life for grand schemes or even frivolous small dreams. Once the strike was over he would go back to picking slate and then, eventually, into the mines; it was what he had always intended to do. Yet it felt good to be free and out of doors on a radiant summer afternoon. He reached into his pocket and pulled out his rabbit foot charm. Somehow, Joanna had got it back from Ethel Dugan! Surprised and pleased, he hung it around his neck. Now he was sure that the Breakers would win.

"Let's show those Lokies how *real* Americans play ball." Boomer Gogarty's stiff hair bristled orange in the sunshine as the team gathered around him at the bench. Because of his withered leg he had offered to coach.

Kevin spoke up. "A lot of them were born here, same as the rest of us, so what's the difference?"

"They ain't as smart. Pa says Slavs have sauerkraut where their brains ought to be."

"Maybe your father's got mashed potatoes in the same place," Kevin shot back and everyone laughed.

Pat wished they had decent equipment and proper uniforms for this important game. Instead, the boys carried old worn-out gloves and splintered bats, wore the same faded shirts and patched trousers that they put on every day. But Father Conlin had made a generous and unexpected gift, two fresh gleaming balls, one for each team.

"Cezlak sure looks happy." Round-shouldered Jimmie Reese stared gloomily at the other bench, where Chester sat cheerfully squinting in the sunlight. "He's smiling because he thinks they're gonna murder us."

"Quit worrying," Boomer said. "We'll beat those greenies easy."

Now Pat wondered. Even though the others were as ragged and ill-equipped as the Breakers, the Lokies seemed more confident. He had watched them at practice, and although some of them weren't particularly skilled, Platek and Wozick were muscular from loading coal cars and could hit hard and run fast, Pochka was strong and mean (he had been fired as a driver for beating a mule to death with an iron bar), and Pawlek was big, compact, and swift on his feet. Cezlak was a double threat as an impressive pitcher and powerful hitter.

"Let's play ball!" There was a ripple of anticipation among the spectators as the priest trotted happily across the cinders, his cassock waltzing at his heels. Behind him, Pat thought he saw a familiar face in the crowd and then he knew he was mistaken; Michael Kulik had gone back to Poland.

The Lokies were first up at bat. Pat, at first base, felt sweat trickling down his back and soaking through his shirt under the arms. "Let's go, Kev!" His voice croaked with excitement.

Dugan stood on the mound, nervously rubbing his nose and tugging at his cap. The first throw was wild, yet the Lokie batter swung at it and at the one that followed. Then, "Ball one!" the priest shouted and, moments later, "Strike three!" With a man out, Pawlek was next in the line-up.

"Get a hit, Alex!" Joanna whooped from the sidelines, but the ball, arcing over the infield, plopped down into the outstretched glove of Kenny Bowen, wide-awake and streaking in from the right. With two men gone, Kevin was steadier. Pat knew he was wiry and had stamina as long as he could overcome his jitters; if he started giggling it would be over.

"Don't let him scare you, Kev," he whispered, as Cezlak shuffled to the plate and stood with thick legs spread apart, toes pointing in, the bat swaying back and forth like a menacing club.

Dugan whirled sideways, raised his arms over his head, and let go.

The first pitch fouled. Chester's second swing made a cracking impact that sent the ball spinning high over the fence and out of sight behind the slag heaps. The Back Street fans screamed with delight as he loped slowly, heavily, almost lazily around the bases to score the first home run of the game. Pat was relieved when the next batter hit a pop fly and the top of the inning was over, 1–0 for the Lokies.

Someone had volunteered to fetch the ball that had landed on company property.

"Hey, look who's going!" Kevin pointed as his sister was boosted over the fence, leaving a long tatter of petticoat on the wire. "I may never see that pest again!" but he kept an anxious lookout until she reappeared from behind a culm bank, holding up a skinny arm in triumph. There was laughter and cheering as she was hauled back to safety.

"That really took nerve," Pat said. "It's lucky the guards weren't around with that dog," but seeing Ethel made him uneasy and he hoped no more balls would go astray.

From the bench he watched three of his teammates, intimidated by Cezlak's fast ball, strike out one after another. The inning ended before he had a chance at bat.

Places were exchanged. Pat put out the first man on an easy grounder, then groaned as Colin Daly fumbled and dropped the ball on the next play. The error allowed a Lokie to make it to second and the next hit sent him scrambling for home. Daly redeemed himself by catching a fly ball, and then Semko struck out. With Zagorski stranded at third, the inning ended with the Lokies leading 2–0.

It was Pat's turn to face Cezlak.

"You still mad at me, Flea? I ain't never been mad at you." The tall, heavy pitcher grinned and hitched up his pants. Then he looked away, taking his time.

"Strike one!"

Pat inched slightly ahead of the plate. Cezlak was shooting close-in and knee-high; out front he'd have a better chance to hit nearer to the waist.

The strategy worked. On the next pitch Pat made a sharp clean connection with the ball, driving it deep and low into left field. He ran, passing first and skidding across second, where he waited until O'Neill, with two strikes against him, slammed a hard hit straight up the middle. Pat raced for third and on toward home, arriving in a long desperate sprawl that sent cinders squirting up in all directions.

"Safe!"

"Out!" The Lokie catcher was enraged. "He's *out!"*

"I said . . . *safe!*" Father Conlin's great nose glowed scarlet as a noisy argument exploded.

"You stinkin' micks got the priest on your side!" Mr. Semko bellowed from the Back Street contingent.

Gasping, thirsty, Pat gulped tepid water from a bucket, vaguely aware that his hands were scratched and bleeding, yet barely conscious of the pain. He was elated when his team scored two more runs and took the lead 3–2. By the end of the fifth inning the Breakers were still ahead 5–4.

"Oh, cripes," Boomer muttered. "Take a look . . . over there."

The Coal & Iron policemen had come back with the dog and stood watching the game from behind the barbed wire.

"What are you staring at, you ugly thugs?" someone shouted.

"Why don't you go play ball with your thieving bosses?" a woman screamed. "That's what you're paid for, isn't it?"

There were more insults, threats, and curses. Stubbornly, the guards stayed where they were, hands on their guns, daring anyone to make a move.

"Come on, now . . . pay no attention to them," Father Conlin pleaded. "You know they'd love to get you riled enough to force them to shoot. We don't want anyone hurt! Let's get back to the game, boys . . . that's why we're here."

Gradually the hostile voices died down, but a sour, angry undertone remained. The presence of company policemen had spoiled the fine mood of the day. Worse than that, Pat discovered, it had ended a streak of good luck for his team. When the top of the eighth was over, the Lokies had moved ahead 8–5, and now some were accusing the priest of siding with the Slavs.

"Breakers ... Breakers ... ain't so swell!" rang out a tough mocking voice. "Breakers ... Breakers ... go to hell!"

"Ding dong bell ... Hunkies smell!" This taunt came from a group from Cork Lane. "Lokies ... Lokies ... peeeeee-uuuuuuhhhhhhh!"

"Stop that!" Father Conlin strode in among the spectators and grabbed one of the pale Noonan twins by the collar. "Stop that silly, wicked palaver, or I'll give you penance to keep you busy for a week!"

"They started it!" The boy pointed accusingly toward the Back Street fans, but the priest only shook him harder. Annie couldn't stop laughing; she had detested pink-eyed Tommy Noonan ever since the time he'd wrestled her down in the schoolyard and kissed her smack on the lips.

The game resumed. Pat's spirits lifted as the first two players made hits. Then, with runners on first and second, Reese had two strikes called against him. He had been grazed on the head earlier in the game and was slightly stunned; since then he'd flinched away from every ball, afraid it might happen again.

"Strike three!"

Dejected, Jimmie went back to the bench and Pat ran out to the plate. Swinging his bat, the seasoned ash smooth under his sweating palms, he felt in touch with the man who had made it, whose strength seemed to flow through the grain.

"Come on, Pat!" Joanna's voice, warm and exuberant, rose over the hum of the crowd. "Get a home run for me!"

Cezlak's great arm uncoiled. Pat heard the stunning crack of leather against wood, and saw the ball soar high into the burning blue air above the slag heaps. Joyfully he raced after the flying heels of Bowen and Shanahan as he followed them home.

It was the happiest mornent he had known in months. He was surrounded by hot, hugging bodies; hands thumped his shoulders and backside and rumpled his hair. When the inning ended in an 8–8 tie, he was sure that the Breakers would keep up the momentum and win the game.

Top of the ninth, with two men out, Cezlak slammed another hit over the fence for his second homer. There was a long frustrating delay. Now both balls were lost in the slag, and the guards were ready to challenge anyone who went after them.

The priest ran and asked permission and was rudely refused; now the crowd chanted loud abuse as the German shepherd ran back and forth behind the fence, barking furiously.

The old practice balls, torn and greasy, were examined by the teams.

Boomer was disgusted. "We can't use these rotten things."

"We have to," Pochka said bluntly. "They're all we've got . . . let's go!"

More arguments broke out along the sidelines. People were pushing and shoving, calling each other rotten Hunkies, stupid Polacks, dirty Dagos. Red-faced women shrieked, tired children cried to go home.

It was no longer an exciting holiday event, Pat realized, but just an ugly contest to prove one group was better than another. The fun, the energy, the thrilling tension, were gone, and the game had ended before it was over.

The Lokies finished the inning leading 9–8 and in the bottom of the ninth the Breaker players failed to score. The teams exchanged half-hearted handshakes.

"You played good, Flea." Heartily, Cezlak gripped Pat's shoulder. "We should play again soon, what do you say?"

Pat shrugged and moved away, anxious to leave the field and avoid his mother and sister—and especially Joanna Pawlek.

❖ ❖ ❖

The teams scattered.

"Wait!" Pat called, as Kevin and Boomer left the ballpark together.

"I'm dyin'," Kevin moaned. "I need a cold drink of water."

"I'll give you both something better than that." Boomer flopped his arms around their shoulders. "I was saving it for a victory celebration, but there's no sense letting good stuff go to waste."

The streets were quiet. A patriotic celebration had been scheduled in the park after the game, but a long-winded speech was the last thing Pat wanted to hear. Boomer's house was attached to the tavern, which was closed for the holiday. "I'll meet you out back," he said and disappeared through a door that was falling off its hinges. THAT EYESORE was what Mam called the Gogarty residence.

There was no garden behind it, just a sun-scorched patch

of weeds with a broken wheelbarrow upended in the middle and a clothesline strung with undergarments drooping across the yard. Giggling, Kevin yanked down an enormous corset and minced back and forth, twirling the laces between his fingertips.

Pat laughed. "If Boomer's mother catches you," he said, "she'll bounce you right into the middle of next week."

Mrs. Gogarty could toss drunks even farther than her burly husband could.

They waited in a sagging shed among a lot of abandoned junk, while noisy bluebottles bumbled around them in the sticky heat. Soon, Boomer joined them, carrying a brown parcel under his shirt. "It's Old Overholt." He unwrapped the whiskey, uncapped it, and offered it to Pat. "Go ahead . . . it's on the house."

It was something Mr. Gogarty had never been known to say. Pat hesitated, then took the bottle, tipped it to his lips, and took a sip. He had never tasted anything so awful, not even the thick malt tonic that Mam forced down him every spring. Knowing how horrified she'd be, he defiantly took another swallow.

"Your turn, Kev," Boomer said.

"Aren't you having any?"

"I can drink any time I want," Boomer bragged. "I want to make sure there's plenty for you two."

Kevin gulped, gagged, and then pointed to the picture on the label. It was an old man with long hair and a disagreeable expression. "No wonder he looks so mean . . . he knows how bad this rotgut is."

Boomer was offended. "Have some more. It tastes better as you go along."

They squatted on the floor and went over the game play by play and inning by inning. "It ain't fair that we lost," Boomer said. "The Lokies just won by a fluke."

Kevin disagreed. "No, they played real good. I wish we had some of those fellas on our team. If we did, I'll bet we could beat Freeland."

"Nobody ever beats Freeland." Boomer dug deep in his pockets and spilled out some cigars. "Go ahead, help yourself. There's plenty more where these came from."

Pat took one and accepted a light. "How about you?"

"I only like them after supper . . . on a full stomach."

"I haven't had a full stomach since last Christmas." Kevin leaned back against the wall of the shed, dreamily drew in smoke, and then exhaled a series of perfect floating rings.

"Where did you learn that?" Pat asked.

"Ethel's an expert." Kevin laughed. "Wasn't she something, today? Wasn't she *something!*"

Pat laughed, too. The bitter defeat earlier in the day was moving off, fading away. He was loose and relaxed. Every time he took another drink of Old Overholt, a fiery comet streaked warmth down through his chest, and he experienced a dazzling golden explosion in his brain. Yet behind the pleasant sensations lurked something that troubled him, something he needed to remember. "Those new balls we lost . . . we have to get them back!"

"How are we gonna do that?" Kevin asked.

"One of us could sneak over the fence."

"Not me," Boomer said quickly. "You know I got a bum leg."

"I'll do it," Pat said.

"When?"

"Now. The speeches must be over. If we wait until dark then we'll never find them."

"Just get ours," Boomer said. "Let the Lokies find their own."

"Come on, then." Pat was lightheaded with excitement. "Let's go!"

They came out into blazing sunlight and crossed the weed-choked yard, ducking under vast flounced petticoats and plump cotton bloomers.

"Say, what if the guards are still there?" Boomer stopped in his tracks. "What if they take a shot at you?"

"He can protect himself with this." Kevin tugged down Mrs. Gogarty's corset, stiffly buttressed with whalebone, and tried to wrap it around Pat. "It must be bulletproof!" Gasping and giggling at his own wit, he staggered toward the street, Pat lurching beside him, both of them laughing uncontrollably.

"I don't see what's so funny." Crossly, Boomer pinned the stays back on the line.

The scorched park was empty except for three ragged little girls who were playing hopscotch on the cinders. High over their heads, a red-tailed hawk stirred lazy circles in the hazy air. There were no policemen in sight.

The boys walked along the edge of company property, staring over the fence, looking for the balls.

"They must be somewhere on the other side of the slag."

The words were soft and mushy in Pat's mouth, like thick oatmeal. "I'm going to sneak in from behind. You stay here and watch out for the guards." He waved them toward a place where the barbed wire curved away in the direction of the mine-head. "If they come back you'll have to stop them."

"How?" Boomer asked.

"Sing something . . . *loud.*"

"Sing what?"

"Something patriotic." Pat grinned. "It's the Fourth of July, remember?"

He left them, moving into the dry scrub at the edge of the field. Squirrels rustled in the crackling underbrush, and he heard a swift signal of alarm from a bird in the bushes. He and Peter had explored these woods together long ago. For a few minutes he forgot what he was doing and thought sadly of his friend and how much he missed him. Then, foggily, he recalled why he had come. Finding a familiar path, he followed it, coming out of the stunted trees at the back of the mine property. Here he traveled along the fence, looking for a spot to break through. Farther on, he found a metal post that had loosened, and he twisted it free from the ground. A heavy rotten branch lay nearby. Throwing it across the sagging wire, he picked his way over without getting snagged; once again he forgot what he was doing and stood dazed, his mind drifting, until he heard the barking of a dog. The sound was faint and faraway.

He was a trespasser invading forbidden territory. In Gogarty's shed he had been brave and confident; now he was muddled and confused. The taste of whiskey and tobacco was sour and unpleasant in his mouth, and he thought he might throw up.

Ahead rose a steep hill of culm, radiating heat. Wading in, he struggled to climb, rocks cascading noisily behind him, sweat trickling into his eyes, stinging them. Breathing in coal dust and covered with soot, he felt as if he were crawling up a red-hot stove. Then he almost yelped for joy. There, at the summit, was one of the missing balls. Seizing it, he stuffed it into a pocket and then raised his head and shoulders to see what was happening on the other side.

A few hundred yards away Kevin and Boomer were talking to the Coal & Iron police. The men's backs were turned and one held the German shepherd as it strained at its collar, jerking and whining to get free.

Below, almost buried in the waste, he saw something round and white and shining. What a thrill it would be to retrieve it, give it back to the Lokies.

He sucked in air, then inched himself over the top and began a stealthy downhill descent. There was sudden hearty laughter, and he realized that Kevin must have told a joke to keep the guards preoccupied. He hoped he would tell them another.

Almost there. Relieved, he scooped up the other ball and dove for cover. There was a flurry of hoarse barking. Peering out from behind a pile of rocks he saw the men staring, the three little girls in the park pointing excitedly in his direction. As he plunged away he heard Kevin and Boomer singing shrilly, "My country, 'tis of thee, Sweet land of liberty, Of thee I sing."

Out of sight, he reached the rotten branch, raced clumsily across it, then lifted it to let the wires spring up again. Screened by the trees, he saw the guard dog lunge over the slag, but a sharp shouted command brought it to a quivering halt.

A policeman appeared and fired a shot into the air.

Hidden in the woods, Pat made an escape, slapping his hands against his bulging pockets as he ran.

He would hide out on the mountain until it was safe to come back.

Later, he found himself alone on First Street, staring at the superintendent's house. Moonlight shone softly on the scalloped shingles and lit the fine lace curtains that were swagged gracefully at each tall darkened window. The Eliots had been out of town for several weeks; all their comings and goings were carefully noted by the residents of the patch. Knowing that the place stood empty and unattended pleased Pat in a curious way.

He resented The Palace and everything it stood for. Prestige. Power. Privilege. Yet he missed his friend; it wasn't fair that Peter hadn't had a chance to enjoy all the advantages that had been waiting for him. *Life wasn't fair!*

An odd thing happened. It seemed that there were two of him, one standing coolly at a distance watching another angry self bend down and pick up an object lying loose in the ditch. He followed the shadowy flight of the cobblestone, heard a thrilling collision, an icy explosion, followed by a tinkling aftermath that seemed almost musical as shattered fragments cascaded inside and outside the frame.

All day he had been running, time floating away from him. He ran again.

In darkness he sat on a culvert, bare feet hanging down into the chilly ripples of the rushing creek. Usually it flowed foul and black, but since the breaker had shut down it had gradually cleared; in daylight pebbles glistened clean and golden at the bottom and the water tasted sweet.

His head ached. He had been violently sick in the bushes, had rinsed out his bitter mouth, and dampened his hair.

He thought about Boomer and the way he managed to manipulate people into doing things he wouldn't do himself, taking advantage but never taking risks. Yet how could he blame him for the shape he was in or the things he had done. He had wanted to be a big shot, drink Old Overholt, smoke the cheap cigars. He had deliberately smashed the Eliots' window. Remembering how high and happy he had been earlier in the day, he wondered how he had ended up feeling so miserable and depressed.

Scared, too. Maybe Mam had seen the outlaw cringing inside him that he hadn't even known was there.

Harsh sounds came out of his chest. He was crying, something he hadn't done since he was small. Even when his father had died, he had clamped his arms tight across his chest, refusing to let the bad feelings go; and when Cal had wept with the pillow over his head he had felt there was something almost shameful in his brother's tears. Yet his own came steadily, heavily for a while. When the outburst was over he felt better and thought about going home. But how could he face his mother with guilt streaked all over his face, knowing her worst fears about him had come true?

On his knees by the stream he splashed cold water on his cheeks and drank to relieve his awful thirst. It was then he heard footsteps approaching slowly on the road. "Pat? Is that you?"

"Who is it?"

The dark shape drew closer. "Mike Kulik."

Pat climbed up the bank to meet him. "Then it *was* you I saw at the game today. Where have you been all this time?"

"In New York. I'm sorry I left the way I did; it was wrong not to come and say good-bye. But I wasn't thinking of anything then except how bad I felt."

The humble apology embarrassed Pat. "What did you do in the city?"

"Worked on the docks. I was waiting for a ship to take me back to Poland until one day I decided there was no good reason to return."

"You must have heard about the strike ... there's no work here."

"I know. There is something else, though ... this important struggle. And I have come for other reasons as well." For a moment there was only the sound of the splashing creek, the sorrowful cries of a night bird. "I have seen your momma and we have talked. She is worried about you, Pat. A boy was seen on the slag today and a shot was fired ... she was afraid it might have been you."

"I'm all right."

"I am glad you were not involved."

Pat emptied his pockets and held out the balls in the moonlight.

Mike chuckled softly. "No damage done, I hope?"

"Not to *me*."

"I think maybe you have been doing what young men do at one time or another. If so, it is between the two of us; there is no reason for your momma to know. Your father would not approve, but I believe he would understand. He was a fine man, Pat . . . and you are like him in many ways. Don't do this foolish thing again." Mike put out a hand and gently shook Pat's shoulder. "Come on, I'll take you home."

"I know the way!"

"Of course. But I want to talk about that game today. Oh boy, how good you play ball!"

Pat sat on the culvert to put on his boots, his fingers fumbling as he struggled to push the frayed laces through the broken eyelets. In spite of his misery he was glad to see Kulik, pleased that someone had come looking for him.

With luck his mother might never find out what had happened that day.

• 13

"**W**ell, aren't you a sight! Where have you been all this time? Didn't you know how worried I'd be?"

He mumbled that he had been celebrating the holiday with his friends.

"That was some ball game today," Mike said. "This boy must be tired . . . I think maybe he should get some sleep."

Pat, who had expected another angry outburst, was surprised and relieved when Mam only nodded curtly, and told him to go up to bed.

The tiny upstairs room was stifling, and he was thirsty and restless. Every time he wakened in the night he heard voices murmuring below and wondered sleepily what his mother and Mike would have to talk about that would keep them up so late.

In the morning Mam was drawn and irritable. "You'd better make yourself presentable" was the first thing she said.

"That little snip Brigit Noonan stopped by with a message for you. Mrs. Eliot wants to see you."

"I thought she was out of town." Pat's head was aching, and his thoughts were slow and confused. "Why would she want to see me?"

"How should I know? Maybe she has some work for you to do. If that's the case, then don't keep HER MAJESTY waiting, just go!"

There was no way out. Mrs. Eliot had come back, seen the broken window, and known who was responsible. But *how* did she know? Pat washed, combed his hair, and put on a clean shirt. His feet dragged in the dust as he walked toward First Street. His father had told him about the Molly Maguires, who had terrorized the coal region thirty years before, committing arson and murder. Captured and sentenced to death, the men had walked slowly and calmly on their way to be hanged, knowing there was no way to escape their fate.

There was no way out for him, either.

"So *you're* the one."

Mrs. Eliot was gaunter and grayer than before. Pat noticed that the broken glass was gone, the porch swept clean. Had he actually been there the night before?

"You were Peter's friend."

Was she pointing out that what he had done was even worse because he had known her son? Pat said nothing at all.

"Your face was dirty that time . . . I had no idea you were such a fine-looking boy." She stared at him with intense granite-colored eyes. "I do see the resemblance to Annie. I'm sorry about the girl . . . perhaps I expected too much from someone so young and inexperienced. My husband misses her around the place. She did have a way with her."

He wasn't sure where the conversation was going, yet it did seem likely it would eventually lead him to the Coal & Iron police.

"I should have spoken to you sooner," Mrs. Eliot went on, "but I haven't been well for some time. We've been away a good deal since this unpleasant strike business began. It really baffles me why people don't know when they're well off."

It was torture waiting for her to get to the point.

"I want you to know that you're welcome to come here whenever you like."

Pat twisted his cap around in his hands, trying to make sense of her words.

"To play the piano, of course!" Her lips twitched with impatience. "It just sits there, day after day, collecting dust. It's no earthly use to us now." She said humbly, "Peter would be so pleased if you would."

Finally Pat understood. She didn't know he had broken the window, and she was quite unaware that he had spoken to her on the day her son had died. It was an act of contrition; she was trying to make amends for the night she had sent him away from the house.

What she was asking was impossible, of course. She had humiliated him once; he would never lay his hands on that beautiful shining keyboard again. She wouldn't have suggested it if she'd known what had happened the night before.

He ought to confess, but he couldn't. Even if it relieved his guilty conscience it would only hurt her more.

Not yet.

"Thank you, Mrs. Eliot."

He turned to leave, but she took hold of his sleeve. "You will come back, won't you?"

He pulled away, hurried across the porch and down the broad white steps. At the gate he looked back and saw her in the doorway gazing after him, tapping her fist against her chin.

Oh, he pitied her. She seemed so remote and alone. The bosses and their families had always kept themselves apart, but now they were even more isolated, terrified of violence against them. Poor Mrs. Eliot, insisting that people were well off, not willing to believe her own eyes.

As he walked back through the patch he saw how much things had changed. When the strike had first started, the air had crackled with hostility, men and women were angry and outspoken, yelling *Scab! Scab!* at men who still wanted to work. Now, the mine was completely shut down, and there was a beaten, listless look about the place. The vital indignation was gone.

Something else was missing, too. It was the fierce, compelling shriek that pulled men out of bed in the morning and sent them home exhausted every night.

How queer it was, that hole of silence.

There was something he wanted to do. Back Street seemed empty, with only a few children playing outdoors, looking sleepy in the heat. He was pleased to see Joanna approaching from the other direction, coming from the hydrant with two heavy pails.

"What are you doing over here?" she asked.

"I wanted to thank you for this." He took the rabbit's foot out of his pocket. "How did you get it back from Ethel?"

"She was hungry . . . she traded it for a pierogi."

"Joanna!" Mr. Pawlek's rumpled gray head appeared at the front window. He had thick black eyebrows stamped across his angry face. "You get in here!"

"In a minute, Poppa," Joanna sang out.

"I'll be on the mountain tomorrow," Pat said quickly. "Can you meet me in the afternoon?"

She hesitated. "My mother's not feeling so good . . . I have a lot to do."

"Joanna!"

She picked up the brimming buckets and walked toward the house. "I'll try to be there," she called over her shoulder.

Next door, Chester was chopping weeds in the garden out back.

"Hey, Cezlak," Pat shouted. "Here . . . catch!" The boy's arm shot up as he picked the ball out of the air. "Where did you get it?" Beaming, he lunged across the rows of growing plants, trying not to step on anything.

Pat smiled and shrugged innocently.

"That was *you* who went over the fence? You must be crazy!"

Both of them were laughing as they shook hands.

"Listen, we got two good teams," Chester said.

"Maybe we should join up, make one better one. We could play against Freeland."

"Do you think we could win?"

"Sure ... why not?"

"I could speak to Father," Pat said. The priest seemed to like him and often stopped him in the street to talk about baseball or tell him something about the strike. Wouldn't this idea light up his big radish nose! "And you talk to the other Lokies, will you?"

"Yeah, all right." Chester grinned, shifting the ball from hand to hand. "They aren't going to believe this, Flea. Wait until I tell them what you did."

As soon as he entered the house he knew something was wrong. Annie's cheeks were as shocked and red as if she had been slapped hard in the face. She whispered, "They're waiting for you in there," nodded her head jerkily toward the front room, and scurried on ahead.

Heart thumping, Pat followed, expecting to find the company policemen had arrived.

His mother and Mike sat side by side on two straight-backed parlor chairs. Mam was pinned to her big Sunday hat and clutched a bouquet of sweetpeas in her hands. Mike, scrubbed and perspiring, was squeezed into a dark shiny suit that was tight in the jacket and too short in the pants. It was his boots that held Pat's attention; stiff, uncreased, and crudely stitched out of raw yellow leather. It had been a long time since he had seen anyone wearing a new pair of shoes.

Mam came straight to the point. "There is something you

must know, Pat. Mr. Kulik and I have just come from the church. We were married this morning."

Pat looked at one, then the other. Then he stared at the framed marriage certificate on the wall, at familiar fat cupids and pink-and-green blossoms. The names Ellen Callahan and Darcy McFarlane, entwined in gold letters, were suspended just inches above the heads of the newlyweds.

"Mr. Kulik has found work as a field hand in the valley," Mam said. "He'll come here every Saturday, stay overnight, and go back to the farm on Sunday. Then, when the strike is over, he'll move in with us for good."

"Why?" Pat was still so shocked he could barely speak.

Mike cleared his throat. "I know this is hard for you and your sister to understand ... but these are bad times ... you needed help."

"Why didn't you tell us first?"

"I thought it was better this way," Mam said. "No fuss, no arguments."

Mike glanced shyly at the woman sitting next to him. "When I came to make the offer I was not sure that the missis would ever agree to marry me. You must know that I consider myself a very lucky man."

"Not *the missis*," Annie said in a choked whisper. "Our mother's name is Ellen."

"Forgive my poor way of speaking," he told her gently. "You must always correct my stupid mistakes."

The marriage was certainly a stupid mistake, Pat thought angrily, but it was too late to do anything about that.

"Mr. Kulik has brought us a chicken." Mam stood up and pulled the metal pins out of her hat. "You children will have a good supper for a change." Her hot blue eyes met Pat's. "This is the best thing for all of us." The discussion was over. She went into the kitchen and began banging pots and pans around on the stove. Annie, shaken and silent, spread a clean white cloth on the table and placed the wilting bouquet in a glass of fresh water.

Pat didn't know what was expected of him. A few hours before he had been the man of the house, but suddenly he had been displaced by a foreigner in an ill-fitting suit who sat alone in the stuffy parlor, thumbing through old copies of the *Miners' Journal.*

He left the house, went into the garden, and slashed at weeds until his mother called him in to eat.

The wedding feast was quiet, except for the polite tinkle of dishes and flatware. Everyone was on best behavior. There was a crisp roasted fowl stuffed with savory dressing, tiny boiled potatoes scattered with dill, and a leafy green salad. It was the best meal Pat had had in months, and, in spite of his hurt feelings, he couldn't stop eating until only the fragile picked skeleton of the chicken remained. Mam looked around her with an air of satisfaction and then brought in a bowl filled with wild raspberries and a pitcher of thick cream. "Mr. Kulik has provided well for us."

Pat hated the way she still referred to him as *mister.*

"You're a good cook, Ellie." Mike gazed at her proudly.

"Ellen," Annie said.

"No, I like Ellie." Mam was pleased. "Nobody ever called me that before."

"I think we should have a special toast." Mike left the room and came back with a dark green bottle. "I brought this with me from the Old Country for a celebration when I became an American citizen. Instead, we will drink to this marriage."

Mam, without protest, brought four thick jelly glasses from the cupboard and watched in silence as he filled them to the brim.

"To my beautiful wife and fine new family. Today I am a happy man. Now I have everything."

As they touched rims, Pat saw Mike watching him with smiling eyes and wondered if he were thinking of what had happened the night before. His own eyes flashed a furious signal: *You'd better not tell her!* Mike was his stepfather now and could never be trusted again as a friend.

They drank. The wine was faintly sweet and delicious, the pure color of honey.

"You two may be excused now," Mam said. "Mr. Kulik and I have things to discuss."

"We'll do the dishes together, Ellie," Mike told her. "You wash . . . and I'll dry."

"He wants to help out in the kitchen." Annie's woebegone face crinkled on the brink of a laugh when she and Pat were out of the room. "That's the only good news we've had today."

Pat didn't think it was so funny. "Doesn't he know that men don't do women's work? Not even in Poland, I'll bet." He went into the parlor and lifted down the old wedding certificate, leaving a blank white rectangle against the darkened wall. Then he went outside and hid it in the shed. Later, when Mam and Mike stepped out into the coolness of the evening, he brought down his mattress and threw it on the floor of the summer kitchen attached to the house. He would sleep there, he decided, until the snow drifted in.

Briefly alone with his mother before he went to bed, he asked again, "Why did you do it? You hardly know him. He's not good enough for you!"

Her eyes were defiant. "I know him well enough. This is a sensible arrangement."

"But I was trying to look out for you and Annie!"

"You're still only a boy, Pat. What we need is a man."

The words cut, made him feel small.

"You'll be sorry. I know I am."

Her face closed against him. Even when she realized her mistake he was sure she would never admit she was wrong.

He had almost given up on Joanna when he heard footsteps on the path and saw her stride out from the trees at the edge of the clearing.

"We have a new baby at our house!" She was happy and excited. "It came late last night . . . and a lovely boy this time, imagine that! But Momma is exhausted . . . I can't stay very long."

They sat together in a grassy space, leaning their backs against a sunwarmed boulder as they talked. Pat liked being with her and enjoyed looking at her. There was a sparkle of interest in her tilted eyes. "So, you have important news, too. I heard that your mother has married again."

It was the last thing he wanted to discuss. "Yes."

"Poppa will be disappointed." She had a wonderful laugh that rippled up from deep in her chest. "Once he had plans of his own for Michael and me."

"That's disgusting."

"To you, maybe. Things are often arranged that way among us, and they usually work out all right."

Pat didn't want to talk about it.

"Michael is hard working and well respected. You should be grateful to have him for a father. He'll be a good provider."

"We were doing fine without him."

"Nobody is doing fine these days." Her fingers touched his wrist. "You do like him, don't you? I thought you were friends."

"We were . . . before."

"Then why not now?"

How could he explain that the marriage had made such a difference? He and his family were linked to something strange and foreign and Mike's slow broken accent and clumsy yellow boots had become part of them. "He just doesn't fit in."

"You mean that he's not an American."

"Yes. He's *not* an American. He's not like us."

"I see." Joanna's warm interested expression was gone, and her green eyes were cold. She stood up abruptly, brushing twigs and grasses from her full cotton skirt. "So you're ashamed of him because he's Polish . . . and that means that you're ashamed of me."

She moved swiftly across the clearing, parted the bushes that concealed the path, and was gone.

It was because he had known her so long and always taken her approval for granted that he had spoken so thoughtlessly, without considering her feelings at all.

What would he do if she never spoke to him again?

◆ 14

"**L**isten to this, Pat. Oooooooh, just listen!"

Annie read rapidly from the newspaper, "I do not know who you are; I see that you are a religious man; but you are evidently biased in favor of the right of the working man to control a business in which he has no other interest than to secure fair wages for the work he does. . . .'"

"Wait a minute," Pat said. "What is all this?"

"It's a letter that the president of the Reading Railroad wrote to some man in Wilkes-Barre who wants him to settle the strike. Now shhhhhhh . . . this is the part that I want you to hear. This is what Mr. Baer told him: "I beg you not to be dis-couraged. The rights and interests of the laboring man will be protected and cared for—*not by labor agitators, but by Christian men to whom God in His infinite wisdom has given the control of the property interests of the country,* and upon the successful management on which so much depends.'"

Pat laughed at her. "Why are you so upset?"

"It makes me so angry!" Annie's eyes were like live blue

fire. "To see what that arrogant man really believes right here in print."

"Do not be discouraged,'" she continued. "'Pray earnestly that *right may triumph,* always remembering that the Lord God Omnipotent still reigns and that His reign is one of law and order and not violence and crime.'"

She threw down the sheets in disgust. "The nerve of him, suggesting that God has appointed *him* the Holy General Manager of the coal fields! Why, he wouldn't know a miner's auger from a mule's rear end! The Divine Right of Kings was plain silly ... but *this* is ridiculous."

"I don't agree with you," Pat said. "It's a stroke of good luck."

"How can you say that?"

"Annie, it's finally right out in the open what these coal barons think. Now a lot of ordinary working people are going to read that letter, and it's going to make them mad enough to come over to our side. And that's exactly what the miners will need to settle this thing."

He was pleased when, day after day, newspapers across the country reported how deeply many Americans resented George Baer's lofty point of view. A conflict that had been chiefly a regional matter was suddenly creating interest in every state. At the mine workers' convention in Indianapolis, John Mitchell quietly persuaded delegates not to vote for a national suspension of mining.

"The soft coal workers have already made an agreement with their employers that must be upheld," he insisted. "They must not go out on a sympathy strike no matter how willing they are to support their brothers in the anthracite fields. To disregard the sacredness of a contract strikes at the very vitals of organized labor." Then he made an important suggestion. "But if they will send part of their wages to our suffering people in northeastern Pennsylvania it will enable them to hold out longer and will be a great contribution to the cause."

Pat met Brian Foley in Cork Lane one evening as the sun was going down, and they talked together for a few minutes. It pleased him when older men spoke to him as if he were a grown-up, too.

"Mitchell's definitely made a good impression," the schoolmaster said. "He didn't condone the soft coal men breaking their contract ... that proves he's a man of honor, someone who can be trusted. It will do a lot to build confidence in the union." He mentioned that a relief fund had been set up and that contributions were already pouring in from all over the country. The depression that had hung over the region was slowly lifting, fear of starvation replaced with a new determination not to give in. "But what will happen when the cold weather arrives? Without fuel the factories will be forced to shut down ... and I wonder how compassionate people will be when their own jobs are on the line?"

"Then you think we still could be forced to go back to work?"

"I hope not." Foley stared off in the direction of the breaker, climbing a streaked red sky. "I feel so useless. I've always been on the sidelines, even in this battle."

When Pat had played the piano at the Eliots', an inner door had opened on hidden possibilities, then slammed shut again. In night school Foley had opened other doors that were still ajar. Awkwardly, Pat groped for words. "Your classes meant a lot to us," he said. "You helped us understand what this fight was all about. You really are a part of it. We owe a lot to you."

"Thank you, Pat." Foley's rare smile was warm. "I appreciate that."

"There's been trouble," Mike told the family when he came in late one Saturday night. "Big trouble."

"Where?" Mam asked.

"Shenandoah. A deputy sheriff was protecting two scabs from a mob . . . four or five thousand men, all screaming mad. The sheriff's brother tried to help him and was killed."

"The miners did that?" Mam was appalled.

"No, someone else did, but the strikers will be blamed for sure. It's the worst thing that could happen now. The governor has sent in the National Guard." Mike sat down and unlaced his thick, dusty boots. "We have enough policemen as it is . . . we don't need any *more* poking their guns in our faces." He looked around him and sighed. "Oh, boy . . . is it good to be home!"

Pat helped unload the supplies. His stepfather often spoke of the kindness of his employer, who had come from Germany years before to cut coal, had married a well-to-do widow with land, and had prospered as a farmer. Yet Mr. Schmidt had never forgotten his early hardships as a miner and always loaded Mike down with food to take to Scatter Patch; fresh-killed poultry, armloads of sweet corn, as many speckled brown eggs as he could carry.

Pat still felt unsettled during these visits, and on Sunday

when the family attended mass together, he felt as if people were staring at them and whispering about his mother and Mike. But he also noticed how many other immigrants had joined the church since Father Conlin had arrived.

"For so long now," the priest cried from the pulpit, "I have seen despair in the eyes of this congregation, and I have ached for your plight."

He seemed so different from the boyish umpire who had raced around the ballpark on the Fourth of July. Since the Breakers had merged with the Lokies, Father Conlin had been persuaded to coach the new team, and he had even managed to arrange a game with Freeland on Labor Day.

"At last, help is on the way! Let us now give thanks for the generous contributions pouring in from your sympathetic countrymen. And let us ask our heavenly Father to bless your weary brothers in the soft coal fields, whose hearts are with you in this desperate struggle, as they stretch forth their hands to offer aid from their own meager resources.

Heads bent in prayer. Mr. Daly, seated at the back, wadded a handkerchief over his mouth to stifle a cough. Outside, bird song flowed sweet and strong as sunshine blazed through the brilliantly colored windows.

After dinner, Mike spent the rest of the day making repairs around the house, hammering so exuberantly it seemed as if he were trying to nail himself into the woodwork. Then he stood in the garden happily planning how to apply Old World techniques to the new. "You like pears, Ellie? Next year we could graft two, maybe three different kinds on that tree at the back. How about grapes? We could train vines to climb up the fence . . . then you'd have plenty for jellies and jams."

Pat still felt uncomfortable when the man was around. It was only after supper, when Mike had left to make the long trip down the mountain, that Pat felt easy in his own home again.

◆ 15

"Shoot to kill!" Mam exploded. "That's what John Gobin is saying. He's telling Pennsylvania boys that they can open fire on their own kith and kin!"

The presence of armed troops throughout the anthracite region had infuriated the residents. Except for the riot at Shenandoah, most of the communities had stayed peaceful. Why had soldiers been sent, the miners wondered, unless it was to try to break the strike? Still, there was little violence; some stones thrown, some hooting and jeering was all it amounted to. Then, on August 29, Gobin, the commander of the National Guard, ordered his men to use their weapons if anyone provoked them.

It was asking for trouble.

"I don't want you to go to Freeland on Labor Day," Mam said to Pat. "I won't have you shot in cold blood."

"I have to go!" Angrily he turned on Annie, who had

brought home the news. "This is all your fault . . . why did you have to open your big mouth!"

"Don't take it out on me," she flared back. "I haven't done anything wrong."

"You heard me," Mam said. "You're not going and that's final."

Mike, who had just arrived home for the holiday, calmly hung up his jacket and cap. "I'm sure nothing bad will happen to the boy." He patted her shoulder. "Come on, Ellie . . . this game is important, and I'll be there just in case."

Pat couldn't believe it when his mother, who never changed her mind about anything, unexpectedly gave in.

On Labor Day morning, the team set off for Freeland followed by several wagons loaded with supporters. Mike was in one of them, but Annie had not been permitted to go. Pat, squeezed in next to Alex, asked him if his sister would be there.

"No. My mother's been sick ever since the baby came . . . Jo's taking care of things at home."

"I said something she took the wrong way," Pat said. "I feel really bad . . . did she tell you anything?"

"She hasn't mentioned you." Alex took out his harmonica wrapped in a clean white handkerchief and polished it carefully, and Pat didn't know what else to say.

The weather was warm and golden. A hot, blue sky soared overhead, almost the color of heaven in the stained glass windows at St. Mary's. Father Conlin perched up front, guiding the horses along the dusty road, with the boys crowded in behind.

As they bumped along they sang chorus after chorus of "The Doorboy's Last Lament"; the sadder and drearier the lyrics, the lustier and happier their voices became. The song, about the tragic fate of a trapper, reminded Pat of his brother.

Since the first envelope had arrived in June, two more had come, both containing money and postmarked from Pittston. In the last one, a dollar bill had been separated from the others and folded in a slip of paper marked "For Pat." He knew it was repayment for the money Cal had taken from him when he left in March. There was no other message, no return address.

When the boys paused for breath, the priest sang alone in a strong, deep baritone,

> "I am a little collier lad
> Hardworking all the day.
> From early morn till late at night,
> No time I have to play.
> Down in the bowels of the earth
> Where no bright sun rays shine,
> You'll find me busy at my work,
> A white slave of the mine."

"Where did you learn that, Father?" Colin Daly asked, surprised.

"At Audenreid, when I was a boy."

"In the mines?"

"Yes, I worked in the breaker when I was a child. I was a driver, too, when I was older."

"Do you know this one, then?" Kevin Dugan, looking as

innocent as when he helped serve mass on Sunday, sang in a high girlish voice,

> "My sweetheart's the mule in the mines.
> I drive her without reins or lines.
> On the bumper I sit,
> I chew and I spit,
> All over my sweetheart's behind."

There was shocked silence and then muffled laughter. Even though they all knew the song, no one else would have dared sing it in front of the priest. Yet Father Conlin's thoughts seemed to be somewhere else as he gazed serenely over the shining rumps of the horses.

"Kevin," he said in a casual way. "I've been thinking lately that the church should be swept out and cleaned up and polished from top to bottom. Would you be willing to volunteer to do the job?"

"Yes, Father."

"Good. That's fine, then. It shouldn't take more than a couple of weeks. And while you're scrubbing the floor on your hands and knees with that terrible, strong, yellow soap . . . you'd better wash out that impudent mouth of yours, as well."

"Yes, Father," Kevin said so meekly that everyone burst into laughter, including the man.

Later, when the storytelling began, Will O'Neill wanted to hear about the Molly Maguires, a name still spoken of with horrified awe in the coal fields. "Who were they really, Father? And why were they so bad?"

"Many Irish came to Pennsylvania in the 1840s because there was hunger at home and the English landlords were forcing them off the land," Father Conlin said. "There were secret societies like the Whiteboys and the Ribbonmen and such that tried to fight back—some say there were Molly Maguires even then—but it was a losing battle and people were dying in droves. It's no wonder some looked to America for a better chance."

Kenny Bowen had fallen asleep and was snoring at the back of the wagon.

"But it was hard, very hard, for those who did come," the priest went on. "You see, the English and Welsh and Germans with mining experience got the better jobs, and the Irish got the worst—hard labor at low pay. Being Catholics, too ... well, they suffered for that."

"But what about the Mollies?" Will persisted.

"I'm coming to that. I want you lads to know what happened before, since it gave a size and shape and color to what came after. Because soon some of the Irish miners started fighting back against the harsh way they were treated here ... but in the worst possible way, by bloody violence."

Pat's father had told him bits and pieces of the terrible deeds, but he had always related the story with a sense of shame that they had been committed by his countrymen.

"It was during the 1860s and '70s that the big troubles began, with killings and beatings and burnings in Luzerne County. People whispered that it was a bunch of thugs doing it, men who attacked the bosses for any wrong, real or imagined. No one knew who they were, where they came from, or when they would strike next. Everything was hushed up and mysterious. There was talk of midnight meetings, secret passwords, and so on. By then, everyone in five counties was so afraid that no one dared lay a hand on the terrorists."

"But they *were* caught." Pat remembered what his father had told him about the hangings.

"Yes, but only after a dozen years of murder and mayhem."

"How did they catch them?" asked Steven Semko.

"It was a man called Franklin Gowen—he was president of the Philadelphia and Reading Railroad—who gets the credit for that. What he did was hire a Pinkerton detective named James McParlan to infiltrate the gang. Now, McParlan was Irish himself and clever and charming, and he swore in court later that he'd learned who the Mollies were and who were their victims. When the time was ripe, he exposed them. At the trial, McParlan named them one by one. Gowen happened to be a lawyer, too, and he was the special prosecutor in the case. Nineteen men were sentenced to death."

"Well, they were guilty, weren't they?" Colin said. "They had it coming to them."

"Some of them probably did," the priest agreed, "but speculation about that trial is still going on. Some people think that the Mollies never existed at all, that it was only a few individuals who were responsible for those beatings and arson and death. You see, no real evidence of any *organized* mob was ever discovered. It was that detective's word against those he accused, and some believe innocent men may have been hanged. They think it was Gowen's way of crushing any re-sistance to the way the mine owners ran their affairs. It's a fact that union activity was squashed for years after the trial."

Father Conlin looked over his shoulder with a smile. "When I was a boy my mother could bring me around to her way of thinking in a hurry by telling me that the Mollies would get me if I didn't behave."

They rattled into the outskirts of Freeland, hearing the bumping of drums, the exotic squeal of bagpipes curling off into the distance. They were at the tail end of a Labor Day parade, part of a procession of men with union buttons pinned to their chests, carrying placards and pictures of John Mitchell as they streamed away toward the ballpark on the other side of town.

Father Conlin halted the horses in a shady picnic grove at the edge of the playing field. Some pretty local girls smiled and waved to them as the boys tumbled down from the wagon, while a band in the pavilion nearby thumped out a Sousa march, loud and out of tune. More people were arriv-ing, but Pat didn't see Mike among the supporters from Scat-ter Patch and wondered where he was. He wished Joanna had come to help whoop for his team.

The Freelanders were warming up on the diamond, lean young men in their late teens and early twenties. They looked tough and professional in red shirts and pants trimmed with white. "Nice uniforms," Pat said.

"Some rich man gives them new ones every year," Boomer told him.

"Yeah, but look at them poking each other and whispering." Kevin stared unhappily at his toes sticking out of his shoes. "I'll bet they're making fun of us."

"Forget about that." Father Conlin ruffled the boy's hair. "You've practiced hard, and I think you can win ... just concentrate on playing well." But Pat felt self-conscious, too, when he saw how shabby the Breakers looked. Again, he searched for his stepfather among the large crowd surrounding the field and was disappointed when he didn't see him. Even though his feelings about Mike were confused, he had counted on his being there. Then he saw Ethel, wearing her ugly brown tam and old gray sweater in the intense heat, and making a nasty face at him. He slumped on the bench, thinking that she always brought him grief. Worse than that, he had forgotten his lucky rabbit's foot at home.

The tall Freeland pitcher strode confidently toward the mound.

The Breakers had problems from the start. Jimmie Reese had never got over his habit of ducking the ball, Shanahan and O'Neill were overeager and made errors; Pat, excitement singing in his ears, couldn't seem to hit his stride. Kevin, still dazzled by the red uniforms, gave up so many runs that Father Conlin replaced him with Cezlak. But, at the top of the fifth inning, something wonderful occurred. It seemed to Pat as if some vital missing part clicked suddenly into place, and his team became a smooth-running, humming mechanism that couldn't be stopped. When it did, the game was over, and the Breakers had won a 7–5 victory.

"We did it! We beat them!"

It was a thrilling moment, packed with joy and relief as boys screamed, hugged, and danced in the dust. Ethel pushed forward through the mob around the bench, and Pat grabbed her by the waist and swung her high in the air.

"Leggo!" Kicking, she struggled to get free, smacking his head with her fists. "Leggo, you! Put me down!" Laughing, he whirled her around and around until both of them were dizzy.

"I saw it!" Mike's beaming face was scarlet. He took Pat's bat and kissed it. "I saw that wonderful home run!"

"I got a single and a double, too! Where have you been . . . when did you get here?"

"The men I came with stopped at a tavern and got drunk. So I walked . . . oh, boy, did I walk!" He pumped Pat's hand up and down. "I saw the last inning . . . saw you fellas lick those Freelanders. What a game! Your father would have been so proud, but no prouder than me."

They were given a picnic supper in the grove. Players from both teams joked back and forth among the tables as some friendly women from the Methodist Church handed around plates of ham and salad. A slender girl with copper-colored hair spoke to Pat as she served him a thick slice of chocolate cake. "You'll come to the square dance, won't you?"

"Where?"

"At the pavilion." Her dark gaze lingered on Pat. "Remember, now . . . you're all invited."

"You boys may stay until ten," Father Conlin told them. "Mike will be driving back with us."

The evening opened, a soft, yellow flowering of light against dark as lanterns bloomed around the hall. Through the grove, fireflies flashed like showers of tiny stars flung in among the shadows.

People arrived, drawn to the glow; gaunt miners and their wives, hopeful bachelors, laughing young men and women, arm-in-arm. A slim-waisted group of girls in light dresses ran up the steps and a gay voice asked, "You'll dance with us, won't you?" as they passed.

"Go on . . ." Boomer gave Pat a shove. "That brown-eyed one is looking straight at you."

"I don't know how." Blushing, Pat ducked behind Chester, trying to squeeze out of sight. A thin, bald man was tuning his violin on the platform, while a fat, flushed one with a red kerchief knotted around his neck called out,

"Hurry, folks, fill the hall,
Get your partners, one and all.
Find your honey, find your sweet.
Get that gal out on her feet . . ."

"Look . . ." Chester poked Pat in the ribs. "That pretty one is still giving you the eye. Go on, Flea . . . jump!" but Pat retreated and hid behind a crowd of onlookers.

Boomer and Kevin had been persuaded to help form a square.

As the fiddler sidled smoothly into "Bird in a Cage," the caller sang,

"First couple right and circle four,
You circle four, you circle four;
The bird in the cage, and close the door,
Circle three hands around . . ."

Bodies swayed, turned, and glided, feet slapped and shuffled across the boards, hands clapped briskly in rhythm.

"The bird step out and the crow hop in
With a silly little grin,
Then those two couples take a swing,
You swing your birdie around."

The strain of the past months had vanished, and the mood in the pavilion was as carefree and high-spirited as the scampering bow on the violin. Most of Pat's teammates had been pulled out on the floor, and Father Conlin laughed with him as they watched the boys stomp and stumble through the motions of the dance. "You lads may have come out ahead this afternoon," the priest said with a wink, "but it's the girls who are leading tonight."

Riding home in the silky moonlight, Pat was as contented as he had ever been in his life. He owed that to Mike. If it hadn't been for his stepfather, he would have missed a day that had been perfect from beginning to end. It couldn't have been better.

Unless, perhaps, Joanna had been there.

◆ 16

"**W**hy *now?*" Mam demanded.

"Because when the strike is over and I'm working again I won't be able to leave."

This time he wouldn't obey if she told him to stay. The frightened expression on her face told him she knew it. "When are you going?"

"In the morning."

"Then I'll pack you something to eat on the way." She was resigned. "Will you wake me before you start?"

"No, I'm heading out before it gets light."

She accepted this, too. "When will you be back?"

"After I find him."

"Cal left six months ago," she said, "but I lost him long before that."

"What do you mean?"

"He was such a fragile little boy when he was small, hanging on to my skirts, afraid to let me out of his sight. He was the one who had nightmares, who cried at the drop of a hat. Your father thought that I coddled him too much, that he wouldn't be manly, but he needed to be near me then." Mam sighed, tucking back loose strands of hair. "Not anymore. Once he got over his clinging ways he pulled apart, and we were never close like that again."

"He just grew up, Mam."

"First he grew away ... then he was gone."

"I'm sorry. I know he's the one that you care about most." Pat couldn't help speaking the truth.

"That isn't so!" Mam was shocked. "A mother doesn't have a favorite child. She has to try to give what each one needs, that's all. With Cal it was love and approval, but I could never seem to give enough."

To the rest of us, you mean, but Pat held his tongue.

"You and your sister are stronger and tougher ... you'll get on in the world."

He leaned down to kiss her. "I'll say good-bye now. Wish me luck for tomorrow."

"Get some rest, Pat." Mam always withheld what he needed to hear.

He set out before dawn, while the patch slumbered peacefully under a tattered quilt of mist, taking long strides as he passed quickly down the lane. On Back Street he slowed; a lamp burned in the Pawleks' kitchen and, hearing a thin, monotonous cry within, he wondered if Joanna was up, nursing a sick brother or sister. Whenever he thought of her he felt sadness and shame.

Outside the village he stopped to shake a pebble loose from his boot, wishing he had stuffed more newspaper into the hole. Another mile, and he was limping again. It was beginning to get light, and he was hungry. His mother had given him some cold potato pancakes. She had learned to make them because Mike liked them, and Pat thought the Polish recipe tasted good.

Wheels rattled on the road behind him. He stepped aside as a horse pulling a buggy ambled into sight. "Do you think I could ride with you?"

The vehicle stopped and a tired voice croaked, "Where are you going?"

"Pittston."

"Climb on, then . . . I'm headed that way."

It was a medical man with an old, worn bag squashed beside him on the seat. Everything about him drooped—his shapeless hat, the sleepy folds of his face, the long, silver tails of his mustache. "Where are you from, son?"

"Scatter Patch."

"Mmmmm. Miner's boy?"

"Yes, sir."

The doctor wanted to talk about the strike. "I pray the men will hold out and hang on," he said. "Gain something from this ordeal. For years now, I've been tending to them, stitching them back together, mending busted arms and legs so they can wallow in dust and water and breathe in poisoned air again. I never thought I did them any favors. Miners live wretched lives, for sure."

The sound of the horse's hooves dropping steadily into the dust made a pleasant rhythm as they rode along.

"I've never been able to figure out why some have it so easy and others have it so hard." The doctor looked at Pat with keener eyes. "Queer, isn't it? How we come out of a secret, live our lives in a riddle, and disappear into a mystery, always wondering the why of it and never getting any answers."

It was almost daybreak. Dawn pulled clear shapes out of the vanishing fog—tall trees, a red barn, the puzzled, drowsy face of a cow peering over a fence.

"Been up all night trying to bring a baby into the world." The doctor yawned. "Well, he wanted no part of it. Changed his mind halfways here and wouldn't budge. 'Listen,' I told it, 'I'm wore out and so is your ma, so you'd better get a move on.' Finally, about an hour ago, he reconsidered. Showed what he thought of us, though . . . came backwards. Independent little cuss . . . I figure he'll survive."

No man had ever discussed childbirth with Pat before, and he didn't know how to respond. After a few minutes his companion said in a voice that was surprisingly fresh and vigorous, "Bless the babies! Tonight when I dangled that little one by the heels I tried to imagine his future, and it was a mighty bleak picture, indeed. Grown men, groping under the ground in the dark, cutting coal . . . that's no life at all." He made a sound of disgust. "But then I thought, as I usually do, maybe this one will make a difference. Maybe he'll pass a protective law someday, or invent a safer device, or discover a cure for miners' lung. . . . *Maybe this one will change things for the better.*" There was a long silence. "A new life, don't you see, is the only answer for despair I've got."

His hand nudged Pat's arm. "You think I'm a crazy old man, don't you, son?"

"No, sir," Pat told him truthfully. "I don't think that at all."

Later they stopped at a crossroad. "This is where I turn off," the doctor said. "Keep on straight ahead, and you'll get to where you're going."

Alone again on the empty road, Pat thought about what he had heard. Babies came along every day, heaps of them, and it surprised him that anyone could still get excited over it, think *Maybe this one will make a difference.* So many never lived to grow up at all. His mother liked to tell how Annie had been still and blue when she was born and how the midwife had set her aside, sighing, "It must be God's will." Mam had a will of her own. She'd snatched up her baby girl and breathed into her mouth, and Annie had been full of life ever since.

He felt a joyful sense of freedom as he walked. A tinsmith soon picked him up and carried him in his cart for several miles, and then a stonecutter with a wagonload of tombstones took him the rest of the way and dropped him off at the outskirts of Pittston. By then the sun was high and Pat was hungry again.

Houses were appearing, getting closer together. An elderly man with a pipe in his teeth nodded in a friendly manner from his porch while an angular, plain-faced woman, watering flowers in the yard, smiled at him as he drew nearer. "Sally won't hurt you . . . she just wants to play," she called as a little black dog ran to meet him.

The terrier danced around him, her pink tongue flopping over the side of her grinning mouth.

"Go fetch!" Pat tossed a stick and she pranced off to retrieve it, then returned and dropped it at his feet. After a few more throws, he rubbed her gently behind her ears. "I have to go, girl . . . just one more time."

He hurled the stick as far as he could and then walked in the other direction. There was a rumbling under his feet, and he had the terrible sensation that the earth was melting and pulling him under. Thrown off-balance, he felt himself sinking. The noise stopped. He was sprawled knee-deep in soil and gravel, surrounded by a cloud of red dust. Grit was in his eyes and mouth, and it was hard to get his breath.

"Here . . . take my hand, quick!" The plain-faced woman reached out to help him back to solid ground. "Are you all right?"

"I think so." He didn't tell her he felt shaky. "What happened?"

"Take a look." She pointed to where a section of the road had collapsed and sunk into an enormous cavity. "They used to mine coal around here a long time ago—it's like a honeycomb underneath."

"Once they took out all they could get, what did they care what happened after!" The old man's sunken face worked angrily as he waved his pipe in the air. "You could have been sucked down and smothered up . . . it's happened before!"

"Never mind that now, Pa." The woman spoke sharply. "Let's look this young one over and then get him washed."

"What about the dog?" Pat asked.

"Lord, I forgot all about her. Sally? Come, Sally!"

The little terrier crept forward, trembling and covered with dirt, and dropped the stick in her mouth at Pat's feet. He was relieved that she hadn't been hurt.

"Pa was a miner," the woman said later as she set out coffee and doughnuts in her tidy kitchen. "Lived with danger all his life. I was so happy when he was able to retire a few years ago. But now look what's happened, and that's not the first time, either. Last spring, a house not a mile away slid into a crater that suddenly appeared one day. The lady broke her leg and was scared almost out of her mind. A while back, a child disappeared down a hole in her yard and was never seen again. *Subsidence*, they call it . . . *I* call it criminal neglect."

When he had thanked her and gone on his way, scrubbed clean and fed, Pat realized that he had been fortunate. Many coal communities had seen lives lost and property destroyed by surface cave-ins. So many mining problems might be solved, he thought, if only the owners would cooperate with the men instead of prolonging the war between them.

In Pittston, he walked up and down the hilly streets, staring at all the people going about their business, at houses, at horses tethered to hitching posts. He stopped in at the post office, a barbershop, and various stores to inquire about Cal, but without any results.

"How long will you be in town?" a grocer asked.

"Until I find my brother, however long that takes."

"Do you need a job for a few days?" Mr. Fowles was short and broad, with an apron binding his belly like a clean white bandage. "The boy who sweeps up and delivers for me had his tonsils out this morning. You should have heard him screaming . . . that is, until he got a whiff of chloroform. Doc did the deed in his office up there." He nodded at a second-story window across the street. "If you'll take his place until he comes back I'll give you your grub and fifty cents a day. You can sleep in the storeroom out back."

Pat was glad to accept, to have something to eat and a bed at night. From six in the morning until seven every evening he swept the floor of the store, restocked the shelves, and carried heavy sacks of groceries all over town. It gave him a chance to question the customers, but while most of them tried to be helpful, not one could remember seeing Cal. When the assistant came back, pale and speechless after his ordeal, Pat still didn't have any idea of his brother's whereabouts.

"You did a good job," Mr. Fowles told him as he paid him his wages. "Now if you plan to stay on longer I can talk to some of the other tradesmen . . . we could probably find something else for you to do to earn your keep."

"Thanks . . . I'll let you know if I need any help."

Something had occurred to Pat and he wondered why he hadn't thought of it before. Perhaps Cal didn't live there at all, but in some outlying area. Each letter had been postmarked at the end of the month; maybe that was when he was paid and came to Pittston to mail the money to Mam.

It was the last day of September.

He went back to the post office and spoke to the man behind the wicket. "Remember me?"

The clerk scowled and shrugged, his bony face almost hidden under a dark green eyeshade. He had a long stringy neck like a plucked turkey.

"I was in here the other day asking about my brother. I'm hoping he might stop in today."

The clerk made an odd clucking sound in his throat and went on sorting envelopes and poking them into compartments.

"I haven't seen him in six months." Pat gave up on making conversation. He sat in a chair in the corner and watched with interest as men and women came and went, their faces reflecting good tidings or bad as they opened their mail. He thought of Annie and how it would drive her crazy to see people reading letters that she couldn't read herself.

"I guess I'll get some fresh air," he said at noon, not expecting an answer and not getting one.

Outside, he stood in the autumn sunshine, afraid to leave and walk around the block or even get something to eat. Cal might arrive and be gone before he returned. His stomach ached with hunger. When the warm light faded and the afternoon turned chilly, he went back inside the building.

This time he paced, back and forth, watching the long black hands of the clock click forward slowly. Then clerk spoke to him for the first time all day. "We're closing in five minutes."

"I guess he's not coming."

The man took off his eyeshade and began locking drawers.

The front door swung open and shut. A young man hurried in, taller and thinner than Pat remembered, someone both strange and familiar. "Cal?"

"Pat!" They moved toward each other, hugged awkwardly, then stepped apart.

The clerk showed no surprise or interest in the reunion. He reached out to take the letter that the older boy held. "Shall I post that for you?"

"Never mind." Cal put the envelope in his pocket. The wicket slammed shut. Smiling at each other, the brothers walked out into the street.

"Where do you live?" Pat asked.

"About five miles away on the other side of town. I'm staying with a nice couple. They'll want to give you a meal and you can sleep in my room."

"I've earned some money . . . I can pay."

"No, I'm sure that they won't let you."

"What do you do there?"

"Mr. Weir's a carpenter, and he's teaching me the trade. He gives me room and board and some money at the end of the month . . . that's what I've been sending home."

Their talk was strained and cautious, as if they barely knew each other.

Walking out of Pittston, passing groups of miners standing idle on the street, Pat said, "You have to know something . . . Mam got married again."

"Married!" Shocked, Cal stopped. "Dad hasn't been dead a year yet!"

"It's not what you think. She says it's just a sensible arrangement."

"It doesn't make sense to me." Upset and unhappy, Cal was walking again. "It's all my fault. If I'd been there she never would have done it."

"I'm sure she thought she was doing what was best for us."

"Who did she marry?"

"Mike Kulik . . . but it isn't the end of the world." Only after he had said it did Pat realize it was true. "You can tell how much he thinks of her, and he's good to Annie and me, too."

"He got me that job as a trapper . . . he must be mad at me about that . . . but I couldn't stay."

Why not? Pat wanted to ask, but didn't. When his brother was ready to give him a reason, he would.

Cal lived in the country in a neat, gabled house that shone with white paint. The front yard was filled with bright flower beds, birdbaths, and wooden gnomes; tiny faces peered out from behind shrubs and bushes, little forms huddled under giant painted mushrooms and danced in a ring around a tub filled with fading geraniums.

"Mrs. Weir loves them." Cal grinned. "Don't ask me why, she just does."

The carpenter was smooth and brown and delicate, like a spindle turned out on a lathe, and his small, fragile wife had a voice that was surprisingly robust as she welcomed Pat into their home. "You like pork chops, don't you? I never met a boy your age who didn't. You can have second helpings, too . . . as long as you haven't come to fetch your brother away."

Pat hadn't eaten in hours, and the meal was delicious. He didn't refuse when his hostess insisted that he have another slice of warm apple pie.

"What kind of carpentry work do you do?" he asked Mr. Weir politely.

"We ain't particular. We do it all . . . exterior, interior . . . and this boy of ours is pretty good with the fancy stuff. He's done some mighty fine gingerbread trim for a lot of places hereabouts."

"People ask him now to do the coffins," Mrs. Weir said. "He makes them so personal—carves some special motif on each one . . . an initial or a wildflower, a lamb or a dove for a child. It's as if he signs his own name with his handiwork, it's that artistic and outstanding." She smiled proudly across the table at Cal.

"He just dropped into our laps one day last winter," her husband said. "Asking directions, though I ain't sure he knew where it was he wanted to go."

"It was cold . . . bitter cold." Mrs. Weir poured coffee from a shining metal pot and handed around the china cups. "I told him he'd better stay over and bed down on the sofa, and that's what he did. Helped out for a few days and then we asked him to stay on. We never had a child of our own, and so we picked out the very one we wanted. And wasn't he worth waiting for!" She placed a firm little hand on Pat's arm. "You can sleep with him up in the loft, but please don't talk him into leaving us. I know how selfish that is, but I don't know what we'd do without him."

The workshop was a building separate from the house. Cal had an airy room above, furnished with an old spool bed, odds and ends of furniture, and cheerful braided rugs that scattered bright wheels of color on the floor. Birds, carved out of wood, were everywhere, perched on tables and chairs and windowsills.

"You made all these?" Pat picked up a magnificent owl and fingered the broad sweep of its wings. "This is so beautiful."

"It's something to do in the evenings."

"You've found a good place here."

"Yes, and I'm doing something I really enjoy." Cal reached out and passed his scarred hand over the finely detailed feathers, lightly rubbing the grain of the pine against his thumb. "I feel there's a spirit in each piece of wood," he said quietly. "That's what I try and set free when I work."

There was so much to say. Easier now, they talked for hours about all that had happened since Cal left home. It was very late when they finally blew out the lamp and climbed into the comfortable bed. Cal settled against the pillows, folding his arms behind his head in the familiar way. "I'm sorry I took your money when I left. I felt so bad about that."

"It wasn't much; anyway, you paid it back."

"I did it because I had to get away, Pat. I thought I would suffocate down in the mine. You'll never know how terrible it was."

"You were afraid to go underground?"

"I was terrified . . . every minute of every day. I felt the walls squeezing in, the roof pressing down—my heart would go so fast I thought my chest would burst—and it only got worse. I was sure that I'd die down there if I didn't go crazy first."

"Why didn't you tell us?"

"I was the oldest, the one who was supposed to take Dad's place. But how could I when I was so weak, such a coward?"

"You couldn't help how you felt—it was nothing to be ashamed about."

"Maybe not, but I just couldn't cope with it then. That's why I left."

"I wish I'd known. I'm so sorry . . . for all you've been through." Pat was almost too tired to speak. "Good night, Cal."

His brother gave a deep, peaceful sigh. "Good night," he said and sank beneath the covers.

Pat wakened to the cry of a rooster, a noisy banner of sound lifting in the early dawn. Rain clicked lightly against the windows, and he smelled the pleasing aroma of wood shavings drifting up from the workshop below.

He slipped out of bed and dressed quickly, then tugged at the tangled quilts. "Cal . . . I'm leaving now."

The buried figure stirred and struggled to sit up. "You just got here."

"Thank the Weirs again for me, will you?"

Cal was awake, rubbing the sleep from his eyes. "You could stay on here for a while. I wish you would . . . what's your hurry?"

Pat didn't know how to explain his sudden need to get back to the patch. It seemed strange to him that he felt pulled toward the one place his brother wanted to avoid.

"I have to go home ... Mam will be worried. But you'll be home for Christmas, won't you?"

"You can count on it," Cal said.

◆ 17

Autumn torched the hills of Pennsylvania. Color licked down the branches of the mountain sumac in thin red flames and flared in warm bursts of yellow around the drab patches.

Cold weather was rapidly approaching. Coal would soon be needed to heat homes across the country. Pressure to settle the dispute grew even more intense, but the operators continued to ignore the demands of the miners.

"The strike will end when the men come back to work of their own accord and on the same terms as before," the press was told.

Nothing had changed.

Theodore Roosevelt, deeply worried at the stalemate, called the heads of the leading anthracite companies to meet with John Mitchell and other union officials at the White House in Washington.

"Are you asking us to meet with *outlaws?*" one of the railroad men demanded.

"This is the first time in our history that a United States president has intervened directly between the forces of capital and labor!" Roosevelt's thick glasses flashed with his swift, energetic movements. "But something has to be done. It's a national calamity ... and I can't just stand by and allow people to freeze."

Yet the conference was a failure. The owners, still stubbornly refusing to deal with the mine workers' union, suggested that federal troops be sent in to squelch the strike and force the men back into the mines.

The President exploded when the meeting was over. "Mitchell was the only gentleman in the group. The only one willing to talk or to listen. He's always been ready to let a third party help reach a settlement, but of course the operators won't even consider arbitration." He smashed down a fist on his desk in frustration.

With the strike fund providing just enough relief to keep them alive, people in the mining communities struggled to hold out a little longer, but they were undernourished and exhausted. Some were abusive, and scared children ran wild in the patches, afraid to go home. Owners saw profits slipping away and public opinion firmly set against them. Like a fraying rope, the tug-of-war between the two sides threatened to snap, with nobody sure of the outcome.

"'They don't suffer; why, they can't even speak English,'" Annie sputtered one day. "Oh, wouldn't I love to see *him* suffer. Boiling oil would be too good for him."

"Who are you talking about?" Pat asked.

"That high-hat Mr. Baer ... the one who said God put the

big shots in charge of the country, remember? Well, this is what he says about the foreign miners. *They* don't suffer; why, they can't even speak English.'" Indignantly she crumpled the newspaper and stuffed it out of sight in the trash. "What if Mike were to see that, Pat? Can you imagine how he'd feel?"

Soldiers had been visible since August when the "shoot-to-kill" order had enraged the residents of the region. Now the governor of Pennsylvania had sent thousands of militiamen into the coal fields to guarantee security to anyone willing to work.

Since the Labor Day ball game at Freeland, Pat had felt easier with his stepfather, and when Mike was at home they usually talked over any new events. Sometimes Brian Foley would stop by, and the three of them would speculate about what might happen next. On Sundays Father Conlin continued to pray for his parishioners and to urge them to be patient and stay peaceful.

Pat had been thinking about something all summer, and one afternoon he walked through the coal patch, speaking to every breaker boy that he could find. On a cool evening in early October they crowded into the summer kitchen, where Mike had recently salted and shredded cabbages and packed the sauerkraut into big earthen crocks. Pat had moved his mattress upstairs again because he said the pungent smell drove him away, but actually he had just grown tired of camping out in the cold.

Annie had asked if she could sit in on the meeting, but he told her the others wouldn't like it, even though he wasn't certain this was true. Lately, his sister had BLOSSOMED, as Mam put it. Tall and slender, with lovely skin and dreamy eyes, she suddenly held a mysterious fascination for his friends, although it baffled her when they came and stared or simply hung around her, behaving in a foolish way.

All day Pat had worried about what he would say, but when the time came to speak he found that words came easily. "Ever since the strike started I've been wondering what it will be like when we go back to work. We all hope the men get something after all this trouble, but I doubt if anything will change for us. It'll be the same long hours, the same bad air, and Blackie Pyle kicking our rear ends whenever he likes— and that isn't fair. The company couldn't make money without us, they *need* us, and yet they treat us like dirt. Some breakers are already organized . . . and I think we should have a junior local of our own."

"It won't work here." Alex was blunt. "When the bosses find out who's a member, they'll fire him and hire somebody else."

"But they couldn't fire all of us, not if we all stuck together; it would shut the place down. And if the breaker shuts down, so does everything else. Things are so bad we'd have nothing to lose . . . if we asked for some changes I think we might get them. At least, it would be worth a try."

"Yeah, why shouldn't we have some say?" Chester Cezlak took some crumpled butts from his pocket and handed them around. Pat, watching as the others lit up, saw the change in the faces surrounding him. It showed in the bleak eyes, the hard set of the mouths. Even if they weren't adults yet, they didn't look like young boys anymore.

"Mike says we'd have to elect officers, pay dues, have regular meetings, and stuff like that. He and his union friends will help set it up. But I don't want to keep it a secret, like in other places. I think if we brought it right out in the open it would scare Pyle more than anything. He'd look at us every day and know he was outnumbered. So what do *you* think?"

There was a long noisy discussion. Pat was happy and excited when the decision was finally made to organize. He was sure he had helped to convince some of the others.

"There's something else we should talk about tonight. The owners say that miners are a bunch of cowards, that they'll crawl back to work as long as there are soldiers to protect them. Well, Mike says the men will prove that they're wrong. John Mitchell has sent a letter to all the locals asking members to vote on whether or not to go on with the strike."

"I wish it was over." Jimmie Reese's thin voice was discouraged. "It's awful at home. Ma cries all the time, and Pa stays away from the house as much as he can."

"I wish mine would." One of Kevin's eyes was swollen shut, the flesh streaked green and purple. "He smacks anyone who comes near him, except for Ethel. I think he's kind of scared of her. I wish he was a mile underground right now."

"My dad can't go back no more," Colin said. "His lungs are too bad. So I have to work, and the sooner the better. Maybe it's time to give in."

"We can't . . . something worthwhile *has* to come out of all this trouble," Pat said. "But if the men have a chance to vote on it, why shouldn't we?" He had paper and a pencil ready. "Even if it doesn't count for much, we can at least tell the delegates how breaker boys feel. After all, we're a part of this, too!"

He handed around the ballots, waiting nervously as some of the boys made quick check marks, while others, less sure of themselves, took more time. While Shanahan collected the slips, Pat said, "Mike asked me to tell you not to let the soldiers get you mad enough to do anything stupid. He says to pretend they're not there, because they don't really matter. They won't change anything."

Francis whispered in his ear. Joyfully Pat threw the scraps of paper into the air. "We've voted to go on with the strike! I knew we would . . . I just knew it! And the men will do it, too!"

Lying in bed that night, he saw their faces again in the flickering lamplight and recognized something he had never noticed there before. *Respect.* It made him feel big. Powerful. That could be dangerous, though. Brian Foley said that politicians and financiers often abused power for selfish reasons, and that was bad. Mitchell was different. Because people trusted his word he was able to persuade them to see things from his point of view, to make some demands for themselves, and that was good, wasn't it?

Life, which had once been so simple, was much more complicated, more exciting. It wasn't just the strike, either. He had never realized that the patch girls were so pretty. They were looking at him differently now, like the one at Freeland who had wanted him to dance. Except for Joanna. He seldom saw her, but when he did her green eyes flashed, and she turned away without speaking. Mostly she kept to the house, because her mother was sick and she was needed to care for the children.

Joanna had power, too. He didn't know whether it was good or bad, only that it upset him in a fascinating way.

For days, weeks, and months there had been almost no progress. Now, as thousands of state militia patrolled the region, company officials waited for the miners to go back to work.

Instead, the men voted to stay at home. Theodore Roosevelt, knowing that winter winds and freezing snow would soon billow down from the north, looked for some loophole in the Constitution that would give him the authority to take over the coal fields and send in the army to dig out the anthracite.

Surrounded by terrible pressure, the operators searched for a solution that would end the crisis and still allow them to keep their dignity.

"Something's going on, Pat." Father Conlin was hopeful as they met one Saturday after confession. "I've just had word that the President will appoint a commission soon to study the issues and make a fair decision."

"Mr. Mitchell's been willing to do that from the start."

"Yes, but this time the mine owners are going along. There'll be a union convention on October twentieth, and, if the delegates vote for the plan, then the commission will be set in place, and the men will report back to work. We're close, Pat . . . very close to the end of this thing."

When the votes were counted at Wilkes-Barre, the priest was the first one back with the results.

"Mam! Mike! Annie! It's over!" Pat shouted as he burst into the kitchen. "The strike has ended! Father Conlin just told me the news!"

There was a fiery celebration, with bonfires leaping in the streets, with noisy parties, shouting, and singing. Gogarty's tavern rocked until dawn with the racket. Yet, in spite of the frenzied release, it was understood that the trouble would not really be finished until the commission had made a final decision. No one knew when or what it would be.

That night, Mike told Pat what was on his mind. "For two years I shoveled coal like a crazy man so I could get a license, be a contract miner like your dad, and earn better pay. Soon I will have it, and I want to take care of this family. Annie is going back to school . . . and you should, too."

"But why?"

"To get ahead. In the Old Country, we were told that everyone who lives here has a chance to rise. Out of all the sad lies it is the one thing I still believe to be true."

"I appreciate what you want to do for us," Pat told him, and he did. "But I want to pay my own way. Why should I be a burden to you?"

Mike clapped a hand on his shoulder. "You can take care of me someday when you're a rich man."

"I'll never be rich." Pat was certain of that; he had no ambition for it.

"With learning you can do better than this. It would please your momma . . . and me. Think about it."

"I will."

"Annie is helping me study to become a citizen," Mike said. "Soon I will go to be sworn at, then I will be an American, too."

"You're the one who will have to do the swearing." Pat smiled. "But this time I doubt if my mother will mind."

◆ 18

"**S**he'll have her work cut out for her now," Pat heard his mother saying as he came down the stairs in the morning.

Annie's face was subdued. "Mrs. Pawlek died last night," she told him quickly. "Poor Joanna . . . with all those children to mind."

"Caring for them and a houseful of boarders will soon knock those fancy ideas out of her head." Calmly, Mam poured out her tea and sipped it, scalding hot.

Pat snatched up his jacket and cap from the hook on the wall.

"Where do you think you're going?" she called after him, but he didn't bother to answer. Didn't she know he would want to pay his respects to the Pawleks?

The day before, Back Street had brimmed over with people celebrating the news that the strike had ended. Today it was quiet, except for some skinny little girls chanting singsong verses as they skipped rope.

A mourning ribbon drooped on the Pawleks' front door. A stem-faced woman in black answered Pat's knock. *"Prosze przyjść do pokoju."* She drew him forward. "Please come in."

The tiny room was filled with people, some talking, some weeping.

"Pat!" Joanna came and took hold of his hand. "I didn't expect you to come. I'm so glad that you did." She wore a plain dark dress, and with her hair twisted up in a shining knot on her head she looked older and thinner, straight-backed and severe. "Would you like to see Momma?" she asked.

He couldn't offend her by refusing. He knew he was expected to view the body even though he dreaded it. Neighbors pushed aside to make room for him as Joanna led the way.

He remembered Mrs. Pawlek's faded pleasant face, her cheerful smile with the missing teeth. The woman laid out on the rope bed in the corner was serenely youthful, almost beautiful, with proud high cheekbones and a straight strong nose. The resemblance to her oldest daughter was startling. He said the first thing that came into his head. "She looks so . . . restful."

"She does, doesn't she?" Joanna said. "My mother was always so tired. She used to say it over and over . . . *Taka jestem zmęczona . . . taka jestem zmęczona . . ."*

"Now she can sleep," the stern woman said in harsh accented English.

Mr. Pawlek sat slumped in a chair with a glass in his hand. Pat knew him as big-chested and arrogant, bristling with strong opinions. Huddled in his grief, he looked shrunken and confused.

"Poppa is taking this hard ... he is drinking too much," Joanna whispered. "He's always been so loud and so sure of himself. Now he won't talk ... he can't decide anything."

"Where's Alex?"

"He's gone to our church in Freeland to arrange for the burial."

A little sister put up her arms to be held. Joanna scooped her up and straddled her over a hip. "Don't cry, Laura. *Siostra* is here, sweetheart." The green eyes filled with tears. "You understand, don't you, Pat? You know how I feel?"

"Yes." He could only tell her what had been true for him. "But after a while it doesn't hurt so much, you stop thinking about it all the time. It really does get better." He slipped an arm around her shoulder. "I want to be your friend, Joanna. I could never be ashamed of you. Please remember that."

On the way home, he thought of the strange thing she had said as he left. "I'm so thankful the strike is over and the men are going back to work ... but I'm sorry for you. You won't ever be so free again."

She was right. He would not forget the terrible hunger and despair of the previous summer, but he would also remember those endless joyful hours playing ball. He would never have time to squander like that anymore, and her wistful remark had suddenly made him realize what he had lost.

What about her? She was responsible for a household now, her father and Alex, three younger girls and a baby, and the bachelor boarders. Cooking, cleaning, washing, mothering—how on earth would she manage? Of course, her romantic dreams of travel and independence were finished, gone for good. He knew what her future would be.

And his? For six months he had been living from day to day, waiting while others decided what would happen. Now he had to make plans of his own—and it worried him.

Could he sit in the classroom again and listen to Miss Bates preach how grateful he should be to employers who thought more of their mules than their men? Should he spend his life in the mines as his father had done, or leave the patch and go in another direction, the way Cal had?

Scatter Patch was dismal, gray, and poor. Then why did the thought of leaving go so much against the grain?

"Are you lost, Pat?" Father Conlin called from the steps of the rectory. "You've been walking in circles for over an hour."

"Maybe I am, Father." On impulse, Pat said, "I could use some advice. Would you have a few minutes to talk?"

"Come inside . . . it's a raw wind for sure."

The house seemed tighter, snugger, warmer than the others. In the front room, a tray covered with a white linen napkin rested on a low table in front of a dancing, yellow fire.

"My housekeeper makes the most delicious scones," the priest said. "She'll have left some coffee on the stove. You'll join me, won't you?"

"Yes, thanks." Yet Pat felt shy. He looked at the filled shelves surrounding them. "I'm surprised you have any books left here, Father. I thought Annie had borrowed them all."

"She passed up the religious ones right off," Father Conlin

said, "and everything else she thought might be too dull, abstract, or theoretical. As you can see, there wasn't much for her to choose from."

They laughed. The priest went to the kitchen, brought back a blue enamelware pot, and filled their cups. Lifting the cloth from the plate, he passed the scones to Pat. "What's on your mind, son?"

"Now that the strike has ended Mike thinks I should go back to school . . . but I'm not interested in that."

"What do you want to do?"

"Go to work in the breaker again. We're going to organize a junior local, Father! We might be able to force the company to make some changes there. By the time we leave, it might be safer and better for the new boys coming along. What do *you* think I should do?"

The priest sipped his coffee and reached for another scone instead of answering the question. Then he began talking about the Anthracite Strike Commission that had been appointed by President Roosevelt. Grievances on both sides would be heard and evaluated before a final decision was handed down. Clarence Darrow, the most famous labor lawyer in the country, had agreed to be the counsel on behalf of the miners. "He'll be calling on hundreds of people from the coal communities to testify at the hearings in Scranton. In fact, I've been asked to speak about the lives and hardships of the people of Scatter Patch."

"You've worked in the mines and you know what it's like . . . the commission will believe what you say."

"If I can arrange it," Father Conlin said, "would you go with me and tell about your experiences in the breaker? Would you be willing to do that?"

"Yes, sir. If you think it might help."

"I'm sure it will." Abruptly, the man circled back to where he had begun. "You've asked me what I think you should do, and I'll tell you, although of course the final decision is entirely yours. What's wrong with following your instincts to organize the breaker boys? You could still study with Brian Foley at night. But sign on as a trapper or patcher or driver as soon as you can and go underground. You should learn everything you can about how the mines are managed. That's how John Mitchell came up, you know. It was his experiences as a laboring man that give him his strength and credulity now. I know him well, Pat . . . I can even arrange for you to meet him at Scranton, if you like. He might find you useful one day."

"In the union, you mean? Do you think I could do that kind of work?"

"Why not? You have energy, quick wits, and, most important, a passion to change what is unfair. Organizing isn't safe or easy, you're certainly aware of that. Men have been jailed, badly beaten, and disabled; some have died. If you think things are bad here, you should see parts of Appalachia or Colorado, where they're even worse. It takes great courage just to set foot in some of those dangerous mining camps." The priest's eyes were bright, and the great knob of his nose glowed in the firelight. "But I believe that trade unions will eventually succeed. Exploitation is an evil that the human spirit has resisted since the beginning of time. And we do make progress. Little by little, we do move ahead in our struggle against social injustice."

On the way home, Pat walked slowly around the skirts of the village, kicking through piles of tattered yellow leaves. He was shivering, not from the wind, but from excitement. Father Conlin saw good qualities in him that he hadn't even known were there. And he was going to testify at Scranton!

Coming out on a stretch of dead land behind Back Street he stood with his hands in his pockets, staring at the structure that rose dark and silent in the cold October light.

It had been six months since he had heard the whistle shriek. Tomorrow thousands of men and boys across the Pennsylvania coal fields would stream back into the mines.

All his life, the breaker had leaned its crooked spine against the skyline, blocking his vision, like something troublesome caught in his eye.

Now, for the first time, he thought he could catch a glimpse of what lay beyond.

◆ 19

The beautiful chamber of the State Superior Courtroom was filled with spectators and journalists, with a crowd waiting out in the hall. Judge Gray and the seven members of the Strike Commission were at the bench while thirty attorneys, twenty-four of them representing the mine owners, surrounded three large, highly polished tables.

Father Conlin, behind Pat, leaned forward. "That's John Mitchell." He indicated a dignified young man who, in his sober dark clothing, might have been taken for a priest himself. "And George Baer is over there." He pointed out the railroad president and lawyer. "He's lucky Annie isn't here to give him a piece of her mind."

They don't suffer; why, they can't even speak English," Baer had said about the foreign miners, but after almost a month of heartbreaking testimony it seemed impossible that anyone could still hold that opinion.

Pat shifted uncomfortably in his seat. Next to him sat a

woman who had introduced herself as Mrs. Burns from Jeddo, her coarse hands clasped tightly in her lap. On the other side, a one-legged slate picker named Allen Rowe gnawed nervously on his thumb. All of them were waiting to be called as witnesses.

Attention was on a tall, broad-chested man in a rumpled black suit who shambled back and forth asking questions. He spoke simply, his style was casual. It was Clarence Darrow, the brilliant lawyer and counsel for the miners.

"You two have something in common," Father Conlin had said on the train ride to Scranton.

"We do?" Pat thought it was very unlikely. "What?"

"Baseball. Darrow's been crazy about it since he was a boy. When he was seventeen and teaching school he even extended recess so that he and the children could play at it longer. He said his pupils didn't learn much that year, but they certainly enjoyed themselves." The priest laughed, but his attempt at humor didn't help much. Pat was too anxious about what lay ahead, and he was hurting badly.

The previous day, Blackie Pyle had yelled that Pat wasn't working fast enough and swung viciously at him with a mallet, striking his knee. Since then it had started to swell, and by the time they reached the city he was having trouble walking. He tried to keep up with Father Conlin, hoping that he wouldn't notice.

The hearings were winding down before the Christmas break. Dozens of miners and mining family members had been examined and cross-examined, and their stories were published in newspapers across the country. All of the accounts had been moving, but two in particular had drawn special sympathy.

Henry Coll, a man of fifty who looked twenty years older, had been evicted from his house because of his union activities, even though he had worked for a company for nineteen years and had endured many injuries. Dumped out in the rain on a cold day in November, he had left his children, his sick wife, and her blind, one hundred-year-old mother to try to find lodgings in Hazleton. Hours later when he got back, his wife's illness had worsened due to the exposure.

"I wanted Mrs. Coll to tell her story," Darrow told the commissioners, "to affirm what her husband just said. Why isn't she here?" he asked the man gently.

"Because she died."

"Died?" Judge Gray repeated.

"Yes, died. I buried her yesterday." Coll bowed his head. "And her mother may be dead now, too, for all I know."

"That is all," said the attorney.

"Yes," said the judge. "That is all and it is enough."

Then there was twelve-year-old Andrew Chippie, frail and undersized, whose father had been killed in a mine accident. There had been no compensation. Andrew had gone to work for forty cents a day, but after months of working in the breaker he had never received any wages; all the money had been withheld because his father had owed $88 for rent and coal.

"You were not getting ahead very fast, were you?" the chairman had said kindly to the child.

So many heavy stories, one piled on top of another into a towering mountain of sorrows.

Now Father Conlin rose to take the oath. Quietly, he described his early life in Audenreid and how he had later answered a call to serve the people he knew and understood the best. As reporters scribbled in their notebooks, he described the desperate poverty and hardships of the people of Scatter Patch.

"Are miners not able to keep their families together?" Mr. Darrow asked him.

"It is almost impossible. Boys drift away to the cities or go into the mines very young. Girls, too, leave school at a tender age. I know of two little ones of twelve or thirteen who slave in a silk mill from six-thirty in the evening until six-thirty the next morning, standing for twelve hours at the machines to make sixty cents. They give what they earn to their parents to help make ends meet."

There was shock on the faces of the commissioners.

"Has Mr. Edward Eliot ever rebuked you, Father?"

"Yes, he has."

"Why was that?"

"He said I made inappropriate remarks about the recent strike to my parishioners."

"And what did you tell him?"

"I said if his mighty friends have a right to organize to keep miners' wages down, then I saw no reason why I couldn't encourage working men to organize, too, to try to raise their own standard of living!" The priest was almost shouting. "That is only justice!"

Cross-examination was brief. Father Conlin had made a strong impression.

"Mrs. Kate Burns."

The woman looked about her in panic, then walked unsteadily toward the witness chair.

Her husband had died fourteen years before, having been run over by a lokie. She had received nothing. Since then she had washed clothes and scrubbed floors, but the money she earned cleaning the coal company offices and the wages her two sons made picking slate had been kept to pay off an outstanding debt for rent and coal.

"Did you ever get it paid up?" Darrow asked.

"We got it paid last week!"

It had taken thirteen years of hard labor for her to fling those words proudly at Mr. Baer and his associates.

Pat's knee was huge and throbbing. It was agony waiting to be called.

"Allen Rowe."

The fifteen-year-old boy said he had worked in a breaker for only three weeks before his accident.

"How did you lose your leg?"

"It caught in the gig. When I was walking to the place where I work."

"Do you know whether the gig was out of repair?"

"Yes, sir. It was."

"Did you get any compensation?"

"No, sir."

Around the shining tables the lawyers made notes and

whispered to each other. Later, when Pat heard his name, pride kept him walking upright. He wouldn't buckle in front of the commissioners. *He would not.*

Mr. Darrow's deep-set eyes were keen and attentive. Frequently he brushed back a spill of graying hair that kept falling down over one eye. How long had Pat been working at the breaker at Scatter Patch? What were conditions like there? Was it cold? Dusty? What hours did he keep? Were there many accidents?

"Listen to the questions, take your time, then answer them honestly," Father Conlin had told Pat, and he tried to follow the advice.

"Are boys punished often?"

"Yes, sir."

"How are they punished?"

Pat paused, trying to think clearly. He didn't want to mention Pyle's assaults on him, he would look like a whiner and a coward. Yet he was forced to be truthful. "Sometimes the picker boss kicks us. Usually he hits us with a stick for being too slow. But only if we don't see him coming. We're pretty fast at getting out of his way."

There was laughter.

"You said he *usually* uses a stick. Does he ever hit you with anything else?"

"Sometimes a mallet."

"Has he ever hit *you* with a mallet?"

"Yes, sir."

"When was the last time?"

"Yesterday." Pat was afraid the lawyer would question him more closely and find out about his knee. What if he made him show it? Quickly he made a joke. "I think it was just a reminder to speak well of him today."

There was more friendly laughter, and then a recess was called.

The ordeal was almost over. After cross-examination he would be free to go. Pat was relieved when the commissioners returned to the bench. He was feeling almost sick with pain, and sweat was pouring down his cheeks.

This time he could barely hobble, and to his horror his leg gave out beneath him as he reached the witness chair. He noticed the sharp skeptical expression on the face of the opposing lawyer, as if he suspected Darrow had coached Pat on how to gain sympathy.

The questioning began again. This time the strategy was to establish how well the company had treated the McFarlanes. Hadn't there been a job for Pat, a better one for his brother, a place made for Annie at the superintendent's house after their father's death? Hadn't they been allowed to live rent-free for a year?

"Yes," Pat had to answer. Yes and yes and yes.

"But instead of being grateful, isn't it true that you've been inciting other boys to join some sort of rebellious gang?"

"I don't know what *inciting* means, sir."

"To arouse. Provoke. To goad into action."

How polished the man was, how skillful with words. Prim, fussy and formal, so different from Darrow.

"I wouldn't put it that way. We talked about forming a junior local of the union, and then we decided to do it."

"Didn't you make trouble at the breaker right from the start?"

"No, sir."

"You didn't complain about how the place was run?"

"I made a few suggestions once and the boss got pretty mad."

"What sort of suggestions?"

"I mentioned a few ways of improving things."

"Improving things?" The lawyer stared at the commissioners in mock astonishment. "How long had you been working there?"

"A few weeks, I think."

"A few weeks?" Another amused and incredulous glance. "You didn't think it was impertinent to do so?"

"No, sir. I was just sort of thinking out loud." Pat's voice sounded strange and muffled in his ears as the attorney continued his questions, using ridicule to discredit him.

"You claim the picker boss is abusive. You said he hit you with a mallet yesterday."

"Yes, sir."

"But I didn't notice you limping before the recess . . . why now?"

Pat was silent.

"Of course, it would be cruel treatment if, indeed, it were true. So you wouldn't mind showing us where you were hit, would you?"

Pat looked at Mr. Darrow. The big man nodded.

Pat bent and slowly rolled up his pants leg. His knee was grotesque, a huge swollen mass of mottled flesh.

"No further questions," the lawyer said quickly.

"I have one," said the chairman. "Has this poor boy seen a doctor? If not, would someone please attend to it now."

The doctor had been kind and thorough. The kneecap was badly damaged, the cartilage torn.

"I'd like to get that boss of yours in my office," he muttered. "I'd test his reflexes for him ... I'd smash his shins with a mallet of my own."

Pat was able to smile at the man's fierce expression. He had been given pills to ease the pain.

On the return train he and Father Conlin sat on the faded green plush seats, thinking over all that had happened. More comfortable now, Pat felt overflowing elation. For a few hours he had been part of the vibrant world Brian Foley had told him about. He had traveled to a big city, he had heard ordinary working folks tell their stories to important people while reporters took down every word. That was something to wonder at.

John Mitchell had thanked him for coming, and had shaken his hand. "What you and the others said today is all on the record," he had told Pat. "I'm sure it will help the Strike Commission decide in our favor."

For once Pat was a jump ahead of Annie. She would only read about it in the papers, but he had lived a great adventure—he had actually testified at the hearings in Scranton!

◆ 20

$\mathbf{C}$al arrived two days before Christmas, appearing out of a whirl of blowing snow. He hadn't sent word he was coming. "This is for you." He tried to hand over a bulky bundle and hug his mother at the same time. "The Weirs sent you a turkey and some fruitcake."

It was an emotional homecoming. Mam, never a tearful woman, choked up every time she looked at him. Cal was strained with his stepfather, even though Annie's laughter and chatter helped fill sudden silences between them.

Later, the three young people walked out together in the winter moonlight. Pat's knee was slowly healing, but the joint was stiff and he lagged behind the others.

"It seems so strange to me now," Cal said. "Everything here seems so much smaller, even the breaker. Not you two, though ... you've both grown inches."

It had been a cold December, and the patch was drifted over. Icicles slashed down in shining swords from rooftops, and the slag heaps shone like ice floes around the frozen shores of the village.

"It looks so clean and white and peaceful." He sounded surprised. "I wonder why I never remember it this way."

A Christmas tree flashed gold and silver in the churchyard at St. Mary's. Pat had seen Father Conlin perched on a stepladder earlier in the week, carefully placing the ornaments.

"You should be doing this," he'd called out cheerfully. "You're the one with a knack for putting balls in the air." He laughed.

Front Street was swagged with evergreens. Large wreaths, festive with red ribbons, festooned Gogarty's tavern and Gruber's Hotel. Only The Palace was dark and unadorned. Annie walked faster. "I get the shivers every time I pass this place."

Pat didn't say it, but he felt the same. With the first wages he had received after returning to work he had gone to Mrs. Eliot and explained what had happened on the Fourth of July. Shocked and disgusted, she had refused any repayment for the broken window.

"I'm sorry Peter chose you for a friend," she told him coldly. "He was wrong about your sister, too. Neither of you is welcome here . . . don't ever come back."

She could still frighten him a bit, but she wouldn't humiliate him again. He picked slate for a living and helped put food on the table, and he would not be ashamed of his rough hands or the dirt on his face.

❖ ❖ ❖

On Christmas Eve, Mam served steaming bowls of mushroom soup and passed a special wafer around the table, asking each of them to break off a piece "to please Mr. Kulik." Mike's pink face was radiant as they observed the Polish tradition. Pat didn't mind these foreign touches so much; in a way they made family life more colorful and interesting.

Early Christmas morning the gifts were exchanged. Mam had made knitted scarves and gloves for the boys and a delicate crocheted lace collar for Annie. There was a shining new dinner pail for Pat, a jackknife for Cal, and a dress length of pretty flowered calico for Annie from their stepfather. When Mam opened her package she stared in silence at a pair of tortoiseshell combs.

"They aren't new, Ellie," Mike apologized. "They belonged to my mother. I brought them to America as a keepsake of her and a memory of Poland. But if you like them, they are yours to wear."

"These are so elegant ... I've never owned anything so beautiful before." She held them for a long rapt moment before tucking them into her warm auburn hair. "Thank you, Michael." It was the first time Pat had heard her call her husband by that name. From time to time he saw her reach up and touch them, and the tiny metal brooch he had given her seemed cheap and ordinary in comparison. Yet he felt no resentment. Mike knew how to please her, and when she was in good spirits then things went smoother for the rest of them. He could only be grateful for that.

Cal's presents were done up in fancy red paper with big

satin bows. "Mrs. Weir wrapped them for me," he mumbled as he handed them around. He had carved a pair of graceful swans as bookends for Annie, a picture frame for his mother, and a pipe stand for Mike. Pat was the last one to open his parcel. "It's a harmonica! This is wonderful!" He ran his fingers over the smooth shining metal and blew softly against the mouthpiece. It was an expensive model, the one he had admired so often in the company store. "I've always wanted one of these."

"I know." Cal looked pleased. "I remembered."

"I can even play a little. A friend of mine has been teaching me."

"Then we'll sing carols later," Mam said. "Come on, Annie . . . you can help me in the kitchen."

In the past, every Christmas dinner had been special and yet the same. This year there were different dishes along with the familiar ones. Pat was glad there wasn't any sauerkraut. He doubted he would ever develop a fondness for that.

When the meal was over Cal said quietly, "I'll be leaving in the morning."

"But you just got here," Mam protested.

"Mr. Weir's back bothers him in cold weather. And Mrs. Weir depends on me to help her with the chores."

"The Weirs! The Weirs! Is that all you can talk about? All right, if they mean so much to you then, go! *Go!*"

"Don't you understand? It was good of them to let me come. They even paid for my ticket on the train."

"*Let* you come to your own home for Christmas? Oh, wasn't that kind, how considerate."

"*Mam.*" Cal got up from his chair, went to his mother, and put his arms around her. "I'm happy for you. Why can't you be happy for me?"

"I am!" Fiercely she hugged him to her. "But it's not the same without you here . . . it never will be."

Pat saw that she still loved his brother in some greedy, needful way, but it didn't bother him so much anymore. She cared about him and Annie, too, of course she did. Why else did she bully and protect and ask so much of them? She hadn't stopped him when he'd left the patch to look for Cal, and her letting go had implied more love and trust than her hanging on too tight.

She was a difficult woman. Thank goodness Mike could cope with her highs and lows, her strong opinions and demands. Anyone could see that the marriage was more than an arrangement now, that she had soft feelings for the man.

He and Cal were up early and had breakfast together. Pat talked about the proceedings at Scranton when he had appeared before the Anthracite Strike Commission.

"Were you afraid to speak?" Cal asked.

"Not after I heard some of the others. All I did was tell the truth."

"What's going to happen now?"

"The hearings have been transferred to Philadelphia; in a few days the nonunion men will testify. After that, mine owners will have their chance to speak."

"We know what they'll say . . . that wages are fair, that accidents happen when men are careless." Cal was cynical. "The commission will favor them—you can bet on it."

"I hope you're wrong. I think you are."

"Don't expect any miracles. We don't have a chance in this fight."

"Mr. Darrow says we do. I wish you had seen him and heard what he said. He cares about us, I really believe that."

It was time to wake the others, time for Cal to say his good-byes.

Pat walked with him to the station. It was still dark outside, with only a few stars trembling in the black sky above the breaker. As they passed the building, Cal said, with a quick sidelong glance, "I don't know how you can stand that place."

"I won't have to much longer. But by the time I leave the boys will be organized. We've already talked with some union men about it."

"What will you do then?"

"I've been promised a place as a driver."

"Don't do it, Pat! You'll be buried alive for the rest of your life!"

There was the wail of a train whistle in the distance, and they hurried toward the platform. Moments later, a locomotive rushed past them along the shining rails as the engine hissed to a stop farther down the tracks.

"Now that Mam's married again," Cal said urgently, "you don't have to stay . . . you can leave the same as me."

The whistle blew again. They shook hands quickly, and then Cal climbed up into one of the cars. As the wheels slowly began to turn, Pat ran alongside, feeling the excited friction as the spinning metal whirled faster and faster. He shouted, "But I don't hate it here the way you do!"

Cal shrugged and waved an arm as the train curved away and was gone.

Scatter Patch was a poor, drab, ugly place. Hard things happened there. Yet Pat sensed he was connected to it in a way that Cal was not, to the good and the bad, the light and the dark. Even in the worst of times, people carried on with the vital matters of falling in love, getting married, and having babies, always hoping that their fortunes would improve, that life would be better for their children.

Wasn't there a rich kind of beauty in that?

◆ 21

"Pat!" Boomer called from the doorway of the tavern. "Have you heard the news?"

"What news?"

Before he could answer, an arm reached out and yanked Boomer back inside.

Something important must have happened. Every night, on his way home from work, Pat made a detour by the company store so that he could look at copies of the latest papers. When the commission made a decision, he wanted to read it for himself before Annie had a chance to tell him what it was. Now he wondered if the report had finally arrived. Quickly, he crossed the street and entered the saloon.

The place throbbed with noisy voices. The day shift had just ended, and the room was jammed with men and boys in dirty clothes, their hands and faces black with grime. Mr. Gogarty's round pink head floated up and down behind the bar as he pumped glass after glass of foaming lager. Boomer was carrying loaded trays around to crowded tables.

"What's going on?" Pat asked Mr. Noonan, who had bumped up against him.

"Dunno. Can't make head nor tail of it." The little man raised an unsteady hand and splashed beer down his chest. "But I'll drink to whatever it is," and he gurgled with laughter.

"What have you heard?" Pat asked Kevin, who was standing nearby with a group of boys from the breaker. All of them looked disappointed. "The men didn't get an eight-hour day ... and they only got a ten percent increase instead of twenty."

"What else?"

Other voices drowned out Kevin's reply as miners shouted and argued around them. Mr. Pawlek, sitting with some Polish laborers, slammed down a fist on the table that made the glasses jump. "They haven't even fixed a standard ton ... it can be anything the owners say it is. And if we want docking bosses or checkweighmen, *we* gotta pay ... you call that fair?"

Others spoke loudly in other languages, eyes sparkling angrily in smudged, disgruntled faces.

Pat felt a sour disappointment, a painful shrinking sensation, as if he'd been kicked hard in the ribs. In his eloquent closing remarks at the hearings, Clarence Darrow had spoken for more than seven hours without any notes as he tried to impress on the commission the importance of their decision. Now, after all the hungry days of the strike, the long weeks of testimony, the almost unbearable suspense of waiting for that report, it crushed him to discover that Darrow had failed, the struggle had all been for nothing. He turned to go.

"Pat!" Brian Foley had just arrived with a newspaper clutched in his hand. "Have you read this?"

The frustration Pat was feeling spilled over. "You told us the strike would be worth it in the end, and it wasn't . . . we've lost."

"I don't know what you've already heard, but you couldn't be more wrong."

"The men are saying . . ."

"Listen!" Foley shouted. "Maybe you people don't understand what's happened here. Yes, you lost out on some of your demands, but surely you expected that. Take a look at the papers and read carefully between the lines. The commission has endorsed collective bargaining. They want to establish a board of conciliation. Don't you know what that means?"

"No!" Mr. Pawlek roared. "So tell us!"

"It's recognition of the union. Wasn't *that* what this strike was all about?"

"Then . . . we won?" Pat was incredulous.

"Yes! The *Evening Post* calls it a sweeping victory for the miners. After all these years you men have achieved the most important goal of all!"

"Did you hear that?" Pat looked around at all the staring faces. "We've *won!*"

Others repeated it, uncertain at first, then growing louder and more confident as Brian Foley held up the newspaper, smacking it triumphantly with his fist.

"Drinks for everyone—on the house!" It was the first time

in history that Mr. Gogarty had made such a generous gesture. There was a rush to the bar and a blizzard of caps whirled high in the air as Kevin and Mr. Noonan waltzed gleefully around the tables. The chant grew noisier, repeated again and again and again. *"We've won! We've won! We've won!"*

Hurrying home, Pat saw Joanna through the store window. The bell jingled brightly as he rushed inside. "Joanna! Have you seen the papers yet?"

"No . . . why?"

"The commission has decided and the *Post* calls it a sweeping victory for the miners!"

"Oh . . . *oh!*" Pink-cheeked and glowing she scooped up her parcels and turned to leave the counter. Then, glancing back at the clerk as he bent over his ledger, she said, "Did you hear that, Mr. Smythe? A victory for the miners, isn't that the most wonderful news? Soon we'll be able to shop where we like and at prices we can afford. Of course, when that day comes you'll understand how miserable it is to be out of a job. You should think about that."

As she swept out of the store she took a deep, shaky breath. "I could have said it better in Polish, but he wouldn't have understood."

"He understood, all right." Pat was proud of her. "Here, let me carry those packages."

"Why, do you think I am helpless?"

"No." He laughed. "I've never thought that about you."

There was the sound of water running in the cobblestone

ditches. It was already March; soon, spring would feather out in a haze of green leaves. He couldn't wait to play baseball again. What a team they would have this year!

"Alex says you'll be leaving the breaker soon," Joanna said as they walked side by side down the muddy lane.

"Yes, in a week or so. I'm going to be a driver ... Mike helped arrange it for me."

"You're getting on with him, then?"

"Yes." Pat saw how much that pleased her.

"You must be careful driving mules. They're so unpredictable ... they kick and bite. Boys can get crushed by the cars, too ... sometimes killed."

"I know." He didn't mind the warning as long as she cared.

Back Street was dreary, the yards still draped with dirty scarves of melting snow.

"Laura!" Joanna took the rope away from the little girl who was skipping bare-headed in the chilly wind. "Into the house this minute or you'll catch your death!" She sighed as the child obeyed. "Now I must fix supper for ten hungry people. No matter how hard I try to stretch the food it never goes quite far enough. I don't know how Momma managed to do so much with so little."

"Is your father still trying to marry you off?" Pat asked.

"Certainly not. Who would look after my brothers and sisters then?"

"Children grow up—it won't be forever."

"Why is it men who always say such foolish things, never women? It's not that I don't love them, I just get tired."

"Remember all those plans of yours? You haven't *forgotten* about California, have you?"

"Why, Pat ... you know I'm not going anywhere." She spoke in a matter-of-fact way.

Even when people stayed in one place, their lives took them somewhere, but he didn't tell her that. He had noticed something that amazed him. "Joanna! You're shorter than I am ... by two inches at least!"

"You care about that so much?"

"Yes, I do! It makes me very happy!" He laughed, looking down at her lovely face. "You'll never catch up to me now."

"I can do whatever I put my mind to."

"Then if I decide to leave here someday, so can you."

"Together, you mean?"

He wasn't sure what he had meant; the words had just slipped out. Yet thinking about it made both of them smile. When he left her he was running, feeling good, feeling lucky,

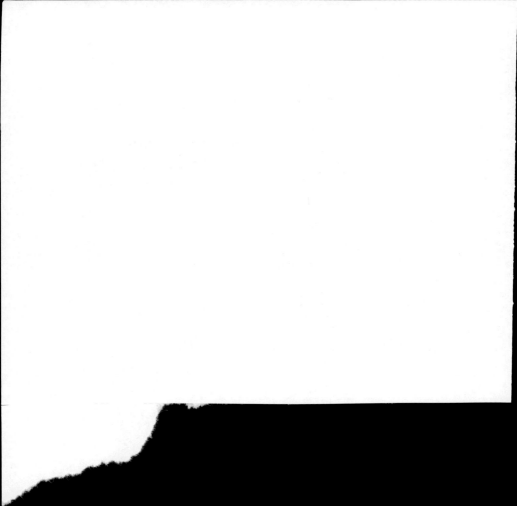

feeling tall.

"This contest is one of the most important that has marked the progress of human liberty since the world began—one force pointing one way, another force the other. Every advantage that the human race has won has been at a fearful cost, at great contest, at suffering endured. Every contest has been won by struggle. Some men must die that others may live. It has come to these poor miners to bear this cross, not for themselves—not that, but that the human race may be lifted to a higher and broader plane than it has ever known before."

—*Closing remarks of Clarence Darrow, Counsel for the United Mine Workers, spoken before the Anthracite Strike Commission, February 1903.*